G000245049

Dead Flowers

By the same author

A GOOD YEAR FOR THE ROSES

ROMEO'S TUNE

GUN STREET GIRL

TAKE THE A-TRAIN

THE TURNAROUND

ZIP GUN BOOGIE

HEARTS OF STONE

FALLS THE SHADOW

ASHES BY NOW

PRETEND WE'RE DEAD

PAINT IT BLACK

FIND MY WAY HOME

SHARMAN AND OTHER FILTH

A STREET THAT RHYMED AT 3AM

MARK TIMLIN

Dead Flowers

VICTOR GOLLANCZ
LONDON

First published in Great Britain 1998
by Victor Gollancz
An imprint of the Cassell Group
Wellington House, 125 Strand, London WC2R OBB

A catalogue record for this book is
available from the British Library.

ISBN 0 575 06508 7

Typeset by SetSystems Ltd, Saffron Walden, Essex
Printed in Great Britain by
St Edmundsbury Press Ltd, Bury St Edmunds

98 99 5 4 3 2 1

I sent my love dead flowers
when I knew our love was dead

For the usual suspects

1

We got to the pub in Waterloo where I'd arranged to meet Ray Miller at ten minutes before noon. His dark blue Aston Martin Vantage was parked on a meter outside. He was early. I knew he'd be early. He was keen to see me and hear what I had to say. We stopped opposite, maybe twenty yards up the street, on the right hand side. It was raining. Hard silver drops that looked like coins and bounced back off the black tarmac of the road. It always seemed to be fucking raining then. There were few people about in the deluge, even though it was a business day, and those that were were anonymous under umbrellas or dodging from shop doorway to shop doorway as if wary of snipers. That was funny. Or maybe it wasn't. 'That's the place,' I said, pointing across the street. 'That's his car.'

The radio had been tuned into Capital Gold during the drive and Albert and Freeze had sung along to all the hits and more coming through the car speakers and didn't improve them one little bit. But at least it showed they were enjoying themselves, which is more than I could say for myself. I hate the whole concept of gold stations. I detest the geriatric DJs and the computer-programmed records. Shit. How many times can you listen to 'Good Vibrations' before your brain rots?

'Good. You've done extremely well, Nicky,' said Adult Baby Albert, punching off the radio and looking through the windscreen that was dappled with water and made the world outside look lopsided. The wipers slapped back and forth like metronomes, and about every three strokes the rubber squealed on the glass and set my teeth on edge. 'When he comes out we hit him hard.' Then he turned his bulk in his seat and looked at me. 'And you can watch your mate die.'

Not that Ray Miller was exactly my mate. In fact, not my mate at all. Just someone I'd met in the way of business. But I didn't particularly want to see him wasted. Especially by this crew. Especially because of me. 'Fuck off,' I said.

Mr Freeze leant over the back of the driver's seat and casually slapped me round the face with his gloved hand so that my nose started bleeding. 'Shut up, cunt,' he said in his horrible, raspy voice. 'Or we do you too. Now.'

I was sitting in the back of a red Jaguar XJ6 with my hands manacled to a metal ring that had been clumsily welded to the side of the bodywork. I wasn't the first to suffer this fate apparently, as there was a rusty red crust on the leather upholstery of the seat under the weld. I wondered what had happened to the owner or owners of the blood. Nothing pleasant, I was certain. The car smelt bad inside. Neither Albert nor Freeze were exactly big on personal hygiene, but it wasn't just that. The motor stunk of fear. Old fear. It was ground into the carpets and upholstery like the smell of too many cigarettes that wouldn't go away.

'Speak to him,' said Albert to me. 'Get him out in the street.'

'What shall I say?' I asked, playing dumb.

'You'll think of something. Busk it.'

'And if I don't?'

'We've still got the bolt cutters.' He jabbed the redial button of the cellular phone he was carrying that I'd used to arrange the meeting with Ray Miller earlier, then stuck the instrument in my face. I didn't need reminding about the cutters, or what Albert was prepared to do with them. They were under the front seat, their blades coated with same muck as the leather beside me. Somebody's blood. Somebody's life. And it would be mine unless I did what they said.

Ray answered on the first ring and, like the coward I was, I did as I had been ordered.

'Sharman,' I said.

'Where are you?'

'Right outside.'

'Is Sharon there?'

'No.'

'Why not?'

Albert made a wind-up sign with his finger. 'We've got to talk, Ray,' I said.

'I'm waiting for you,' he replied.

'Not in there. Out here.'

'Is something wrong?'

'No. It's fine. Come out. I'll pick you up.'

'OK,' he said and cut me off. I felt like Judas.

I looked over the road. The door to the pub opened and Ray appeared. He was wearing a mackintosh that made him look twice his size.

'There he is,' said Freeze, and Adult Baby Albert tossed the phone in Freeze's lap, reached under his coat and pulled out the Hämmerli .22. Freeze restarted the engine as Ray stopped at the kerb looking for me.

He scoped the street through the downpour looking for my car, as Freeze snorted, slapped the Jag into gear, put his foot down hard on the gas and with a scream of rubber from the drive wheels drove straight across the road. He slammed on the brakes a moment later and the big car rocked to a halt on its springs as Albert rolled down the electric window, poked the silenced target pistol through the gap and calmly fired three times. I saw the bullets whack into the material of Ray's coat and the expression of surprise on his face as he staggered back and fell on the wet pavement where the rain lashed down on to his still body. Freeze hit the accelerator again and the big motor fishtailed away, leaving Ray lying there, almost before anyone noticed what had happened.

'Well done, Albert,' said Freeze, as the car skidded round the first left-hand corner we came to, almost clipping a post office van parked there. 'One more under the belt.'

'You bastards,' I said as I fought to keep from sliding on to the floor. 'You didn't give him a chance.'

'You were the one spoke to him on the phone,' said Albert. 'You stitched him up to protect your own skin. But it's not going to save you. You still have to die.'

I said nothing. He was right, of course.

'See, Freeze,' Albert went on, 'people will do anything to hang on to a few more precious moments of life. Anything. Betray. Lie. Cheat. Steal. Humanity. I have no time for it.'

'That's obvious, you fat sack of shit,' I said.

Albert leant round again and pointed the gun at my head. 'Shut up, Nicky,' he said, 'or you won't even live another minute.'

I shut up and watched the rain outside the car as we sped down the Old Kent Road and, not for the first time, wondered why the hell I did what I did.

2

It was raining when it all started, and it was raining when it all ended. It rained a lot that spring and summer, although every time I turned on the TV, or switched on the radio, or picked up a newspaper, there were dark warnings of drought and global warming. But it seemed to rain a lot to me. Maybe I was in a parallel universe. Come to think of it now, I'm sure I was. It was the strangest time I've ever known, and believe me I've known some. Dark days of storms and floods and people who had stepped from a nightmare. And other people too. Decent people who needed my help, and the ones who saved my life.

Take my friend Charlie, for instance.

Charlie the mechanic who'd become Charlie the used-car guy and had supplied me with a long stream of motors over the years, some of which had ended up in the great used-car lot in the sky, mainly, sad to say, due to my carelessness, and the way I earned my living. If you could call it living.

One afternoon a couple of months back he'd given me a call.

'If this is about my outstanding bill—' I said.

'Forget the bill,' he interrupted.

'What? Permanently?'

'No. Not permanently. Just temporarily. I need to talk to you.'

'What about?'

'I can't tell you over the phone. You doing anything tonight?'

'Nothing special.'

'How about a bevvy?'

'Sounds OK. Where?'

'You know that little bar in Brixton. Back of the town hall.'

'Sure I know it.'

'I'll be there round seven.'

'OK, Charles,' I said. 'I'll see you there.'

I got to the bar at the designated hour; Charlie was sitting at a table in the raised area at the back listening to Count Suckle on the sound system and staring at Sheryl Crow on the big screen TV with the sound turned down. I got two bottles of Bud from the bar and joined him. He looked unhappy, all wrapped up in his sheepskin coat like a teddy bear who'd just been abandoned by its owner. 'Hello, Charlie,' I said, plonking a beer bottle down next to its twin in front of him and hauling out my Silk Cut. 'What's new? You look pissed off. Did you get beat up on a deal for a nearly new Range Rover Vogue?'

'You won't believe me if I tell you,' he said, tearing his eyes away from Sheryl and clinking bottles with me.

'Try me,' I said.

'It's difficult, Nick.' The record changed to a live B. B. King cut. Someone in the bar had great taste in music, if a lousy taste in TV.

'It is about my bill, isn't it? Look, I'll give you a post-dated—'

'Will you shut up about your bloody bill.'

'It's the first time I've ever heard you say that.'

He put one hand to his forehead and sighed and I knew something was up but couldn't for the life of me think what it could be. 'Is it Ginny?' I asked. Ginny being Charlie's wife of many years. 'The kids?'

'No. Yes. Sort of.' He sighed again.

'Or none of the above,' I said, trying to lighten his mood. 'What is it?'

'Nick. I reckon you're my best friend.' It's weird when people say that sort of thing. I've always thought of Charlie as a good mate. But not my *best* friend, if you know what I mean. I was flattered, but a little alarmed. I had a horrible feeling he was going to tell me he was dying of some sort of terrible disease. 'And I've got no one else to talk to,' he continued.

Christ. Here it comes I thought.

He took a big breath. 'See. I'm gay, Nick.'

It went right past me the first time. I thought I'd misheard. 'Do what?' I said.

'I'm gay.'

'That's what I thought you said. It's a wind-up, right?'

'No wind-up.'

I didn't know whether to laugh or cry. 'Charlie,' I said, 'I've known you how long? Twenty years? More? I went to your wedding. I've seen your kids grow up. Now you're telling me you're gay. I don't believe it.'

'Why not, Nick? Can't you handle it?'

B. B. King faded out and 'Rocket 88' by Jackie Brenston thudded on. I had to try and get a copy of this tape. 'You're serious,' I said.

'At last.'

'I don't know what to say, Charlie. How long have you known?'

'Since I was about eight years old. But I've only admitted it to myself over the last year or so.'

'You're not having an affair?'

'You sound shocked, Nick. How many affairs did you have when you were married to Laura?'

'That was different.'

'Why? Because they weren't with men.'

There was no answer to that. 'Are you?' I asked again and lit another cigarette.

'No.'

'So what's the problem?'

'Don't be fucking stupid, Nick. What do you think the problem is? I want to have an affair. That's the problem.'

'With anyone in particular?'

He shook his head. 'No. I'm not stupid, Nick. I know the risks. All the risks. Want another drink?'

'Sure,' I replied. 'Jack Daniel's and Coke. Large one. In fact, make it a triple.'

He got up and went to the bar, I listened to Jackie Brenston and then Otis Redding and Carla Thomas's version of 'Knock On Wood' after him.

When Charlie came back I said, 'Does Ginny know?'

'Christ no. Can you imagine?'

'I don't want to.'

'Nor do I.'

'So what are you going to do?'

'Get drunk with you.'

'Bloody good idea,' I said.

3

We did get drunk that night. Drunk like the old times when we didn't have a care in the world except where the next drink was coming from.

'What am I going to do?' Charlie asked me sometime through the fourth large Grouse he was drinking by then.

'What do you want to do?' I asked.

'Stop living a lie every day.'

'Jesus, Charlie,' I said. 'We all live lies some of the time. Some of us all of the time.'

He didn't answer that one.

After a few more drinks, which mostly we swallowed in silence, he seemed to cheer up a bit. Or maybe I was misreading the situation. I was matching him glass for glass, and I'd long ago lost count of how many we'd sunk.

'You know what, Nick,' he said after a bit.

'What?'

'I can't tell you.'

'What?'

'Jesus, but it's strange.'

'What? Come on, Charlie, spit it out.'

'I reckon I'd rather be a lesbian,' he said.

'What?' I said again through the alcohol fumes. 'You want a sex change now?'

We both laughed. 'No. Don't be fucking stupid. I just reckon of all the options it's the best one.'

'Why?'

'Easy,' he replied and ticked the answers off on his fingers.

'One. You get to eat pussy and get your pussy eaten. That must be like a blow job. What do you reckon?'

I admitted it had never crossed my mind.

'Right. Two. You get to play with tits. Now that can't be bad.'

'You're not sounding very gay to me so far, Charlie,' I ventured.

'I know. But don't forget I've been pretending to be straight for more than thirty years. Some of it must rub off. Right?'

I agreed he had a point.

'Then you can admit to liking dick, 'cos you're a woman. Right?'

I nodded.

'Where was I?' he asked, looking a little confused and calling to the bar for another round.

'That was three, I think,' I said.

'Right. Three. No, four. There's no shame in being penetrated. Right.'

I was beginning to feel a little uncomfortable, but nodded agreement nevertheless.

'And you don't have to get into all the macho shit that men have to. You can just lie back in silk knickers and chill out.' The young woman who delivered our drinks gave us both an odd look which he didn't see.

'It's a point of view,' I said when she'd gone.

'But not one you really agree with.'

'No.'

'I thought not.'

'You are what you are, Charlie,' I said.

'That's just the point.' He thumped the table. 'I'm not.'

'You'll always be my mate though,' I said.

'Will I? Look at you. You're as embarrassed as fuck.'

'It's just a shock, that's all.'

'Is it?'

'Sure it is.'

'What am I going to do, Nick?' he asked. 'Come out and fuck up my family or carry on like I'm doing and feeling as miserable as sin all the time.'

'I can't help you with that one, Charlie,' I replied. 'I'm sorry.'

'Not half as sorry as I am. I could always kill myself, I suppose.'

'That's bollocks and you know it,' I said. 'Don't give me that crap or I'll lose my patience.'

'Always there with an understanding word, eh, Nick?' he said, and I could see the misery in his face but to my detriment I ignored it.

My lack of understanding would come back to haunt me.

And that's more or less where we left it. I couldn't help Charlie, but I could help the next person who came looking for me. Or at least I thought I could, and if it hadn't been for what Charlie had told me, and what happened later, maybe I never would have.

4

I'd just got back from Aberdeen and reopened the office when I met Ray Miller. I'd been visiting my daughter, Judith, who was living in Scotland with her solicitor's family until she decided what to do with her life. She was a rich girl now, or she would be in a couple of years' time when she reached her majority. Her deceased mother and stepfather had seen to that when they perished with her little half-brother on a freezing day just before the previous Christmas at O'Hare airport in Chicago. But right now she was getting ready to do her GCSEs. Then she'd decide if she wanted to do 'A' levels, or Highers as they call them up there, and maybe go on to university. Or maybe she wouldn't. Or decide if maybe she'd move back down to London with me, or maybe she wouldn't. She wasn't too sure. Not about that, and not about a lot of other things. And after what she'd been through I couldn't blame her. One thing *was* for sure. It was better that she stayed away from me for a while. I wasn't even certain that she loved me any more, not after what she'd had to do to save my life. Kill a man. Not that he was much of a man, and for sure he'd've killed me if she'd let him live. And then her afterwards. After he'd had his fun with her. Because he was that kind of man. But she'd lost something that day, and if it included her love for me, so be it. I knew that I loved her, loved her more than life itself. But like so many other women I'd known and loved, and who'd loved me back, she was better off without me. When I'd left we'd held each other tightly at the airport, but I didn't know when or, quite frankly, if I'd ever see her again.

I stroked her blonde hair in the quiet of the airport terminal as geezers in kilts and other geezers in big white Stetson hats passed by us. 'I'm going to miss you,' I said.

'I'm going to miss you too, Dad.' At least she hadn't started calling me Nick yet.

'Are you sure you're all right with the Condies?' That was the name of her solicitor's family.

'Course I am.' She said it with the kind of tone that made me feel stupid.

'And you don't need anything.'

'Nothing at all.'

Not even me, I thought. 'You'll call me,' I said.

'Don't I always?'

She did, as a matter of fact. Either on Saturday afternoon or Sunday night. But I knew that sometimes it was more of a duty than a pleasure, and sometimes she had little to say so the lines just hummed in my ear. 'Sure you do,' I said. I couldn't think of anything else to say and they called my flight for the second time.

'You'll miss your plane.'

'No I won't.'

'Dad, you'd better go.'

I picked up my battered leather bag. 'OK then.'

'OK.'

'Good luck with your exams.'

'Thanks.'

I kissed her and she looked so much like her mother I almost broke up. 'Come visit,' I said.

'I will.'

''Bye then,' and I touched her hand, turned and walked away. At the gate I looked back, but she'd gone. Children. Who'd have 'em?

5

So I went back to work. Well, I wandered down and sat in my office and read the paper every day. I had a few quid in the bank so I wasn't desperate to get out on the mean streets again. In fact, I could quite happily have stayed indoors for the rest of my life catching up on old comedy shows on satellite TV. But I knew how Judith felt about me wasting my time, so I reckoned I had to at least make an effort. I still cared about what she thought of me, and I knew I always would.

Then on the afternoon of the second Tuesday I was back, after a liquid lunch in the pub opposite, I got a new client.

He turned up in a dark blue Aston Martin Vantage on that year's plate that made every other car in the road, and probably the whole area, look like trash. He parked it up outside my office, helped a small boy out of the passenger seat, checked the number on the door, and came right inside. It was pouring with rain that afternoon and sheet lightning lit up the streets and thunder boomed so loudly I thought the roof might cave in. As they hustled across the pavement I noticed that the man limped. Join the club, I thought.

He was small and tough-looking, wearing grey sweats and brand-new Reeboks that were dappled with wet spots from the weather. The boy was pretty and blond with big blue eyes. I assumed they were father and son, and the boy must've got his looks from the other side of the family. 'Are you Nick Sharman?' the man asked as he wiped rain from his face and closed my office door behind him. He had an estuary accent, close-cropped hair and a nasty rash across his nose. He looked a bit like Aldo Ray, if anyone in the world remembers what Aldo Ray looked like. I told you. I watch too much TV.

'That's me,' I said, although I wished I could deny it, and almost did for a second. I sensed trouble, but I don't always trust my senses. You'd think I'd've learned by now.

'My name's Ray. Ray Miller. I need your help,' he said. Coincidence. The Ray bit.

'Sit down, Mr Miller,' I invited. I'm always polite to people who drive that much motor car. And, incidentally, look that tough.

He did as I bade him, perching the boy on his knee where he wriggled like a monkey for a bit before he settled down and looked at me with those big blue eyes. 'You're the private detective,' he said. The man, that is, not the boy.

'That's right,' I replied. 'What can I do for you?'

'I'm looking for my wife. I want you to find her for me.'

Another missing person, I thought. Another load of grief. I'm getting too old for that lark.

'Have you been to the police?' I asked.

'Sure. I went there when she left. They told me she was a big girl and could do what she wanted. I made them take down her details but they never got back to me.'

'Salvation Army?'

'Do me a favour. She wasn't off to live rough or in a hostel.'

Right then I didn't ask what she *did* leave for. That would come later. Right then I was still looking for reasons to make him go away and leave me alone.

'I don't know,' I said. 'I don't know if I want to take on a complex case like yours.'

'Why complex?' he asked.

'It's a big town, Mr Miller,' I replied. 'What makes you think I can do it?' I just wished he'd disappear so that I could get back to the newspaper and, if I wanted a challenge, do the quick crossword.

'I dunno,' he said. 'I asked around. I've got a few mates local.' I just bet he had. And I was willing to bet they weren't nice ones.

'Where do you come from then?' I asked.

'Essex. Romford. But I'm moving.'

Not a bad idea, I thought, but I said nothing. Essex people are very proprietorial about their county. 'So tell me,' I said, 'about your wife.'

Though really, all I wanted him to do was get back into his expensive car, head east for Essex and never bother me again.

The boy finally managed to slide off his father's knee and went and stood in the doorway, jiggling from foot to foot and clocking the real estate outside through the silver rain that kept falling as the lightning flashed and the thunder roared. But he didn't flinch. Just kept looking. I liked that. 'You stay in here, Liam,' said Ray. 'Don't get wet.' Then to me. 'He's nearly four. Terrible age.'

'I've got a girl,' I said. 'Teenager. Believe me, it doesn't get any better.'

'So I've heard.'

'Tell me about your wife,' I went on, once we'd got that little bit of personal history sorted, and I knew he wasn't going to go away.

'She left me just over a year ago; came to south London I think.'

'Why did she leave?'

'Money problems. And the boy. She couldn't cope.'

'Money problems,' I said. 'What? Couldn't you afford to valet the motor that week?'

He looked over his shoulder, out of the rain-streaked window, at the Aston Martin that sat at the kerb like a beast waiting to be woken from a long sleep and kill a few peasants.

'That was then,' he said almost shyly. 'This is now. I had a result. A good result.'

I cocked my head in a listening pose.

'Lottery,' he explained. 'All six numbers on a double rollover week.'

'How much?' I asked.

'Me and someone else split twenty-four million.'

'Twelve million,' I breathed as if he couldn't do the sum.

He nodded. 'So you see, my money problems are over now, and I want Sharon back. Me and Liam. We both want her back. So's that we can be a family again.'

I thought about families, and my lack of one, and I couldn't fault him on that.

'Please help me,' he said. 'Us.'

6

'Your wife's name is Sharon,' I said. More for something to say than anything else. I was thinking that maybe I should start doing the lottery. I imagined what I could do with twelve million quid. Open a branch of my office in Mayfair maybe.

'That's right,' he replied.

'So tell me about her.'

'She's a lot younger than me. Only eighteen when we met. A party girl. We started going out, then I asked her to marry me. I was surprised when she said yes. Then she got pregnant with Liam. That's it really.'

'Except she left you.'

He nodded.

'So how old is she now?'

'Twenty-six, but she doesn't look it. Or she didn't. I've got some photos of her.' He went into the pocket of his sweats and brought out a Kodak folder that he put on the table.

I picked it up and squinted inside. There were a dozen prints taken at different times. She was good-looking, blonde, a bit tarty, but looked like a laugh, if that was what you wanted. And she did appear young. And Liam *had* got his features from her. Right down to the big blue eyes. 'She's a real looker,' he said.

'I see what you mean,' I replied. 'When were these taken?'

'About fifteen months ago.'

'So what happened?'

'I'm a builder. Contractor. Or I was. I started my business when I got out of the army. That's where this happened.' He slapped his leg. 'Falklands. I was in the paras. NCO. First into Goose Green. I collected a few ounces of shrapnel in my leg and was medivacced out. Just as well I was wearing a flak jacket, otherwise I wouldn't have made it out at all. As it was, my war lasted precisely twenty-nine minutes.' He laughed at that, but there wasn't much humour in it. 'I kept the jacket as a souvenir, along with my limp. And a few medals, of course. Young and stupid, Mr Sharman. Young and stupid. I got a medical discharge and a few bob. Not much, but enough to get started in the trade. Conversions mainly. Things were all right at the beginning. More than all right, as it goes, so I expanded. Took on more men and bought some development land and started putting up new houses. The eighties. Remember them?' I remembered them, but not with fondness. 'But the recession hit and I went broke,' he went on. 'Had to lay the boys off. That was the worst bit. Me and Sharon had a flat in Romford. Only a small one. I've just sold it. Made a bloody profit too. Talk about money going to money.' He gave another mirthless laugh. 'But it suited us at the time. You see I ploughed all the capital back into the business. Then one day it was gone. The lot. So I was on the dole. I didn't like that. I prefer getting my hands dirty, but there was no work. She was OK when she was pregnant. It pulled us together really.' He looked round at Liam and lowered his voice in deference to him, but I don't think the kid was listening. He was more interested in studying a half-drowned pigeon with one leg hopping across a puddle in the pavement. 'But he can be a bit of a handful. She couldn't cope. I got a few foreigners away, doing the work myself. For cash, you know.'

I knew.

'She started leaving Liam with her mum and . . .' He paused and looked a bit sick.

'Yeah?'

'She started going down the clubs again. That's where I met her. The Hollywood.'

'Other blokes?' I asked.

He looked round at the boy again, then looked back at me and nodded. 'It wasn't her fault,' he said sadly. 'She's not a bad girl. Just easily led. She likes a good time and I couldn't give it to her. Couldn't afford to. Not then.'

I wondered how many times I'd heard that or something similar before?

'And then one day she didn't come back,' he continued.

'Rough,' I said.

'But now I'm buying a new place. Out past the M25. In the country. It'll be good for the boy. Her mum's moving in to look after him. Christ, I'll get a nanny if Sharon wants one. A cook.'

'A butler,' I said.

He checked to see if I was taking the piss. 'If she wants one. I'm rich, and I want you to find her.'

'What exactly makes you think she's round here?'

'She was knocking about with one particular fella.'

'That makes it complicated. If it's love.'

'She can't love him. She loves me.'

Sure, I thought, they always do. And how many times had I heard that one before too? 'Who's the bloke?' I asked.

'His name's Chris Grant,' he said. 'She used to go clubbing with a bird called Melanie. She told me about him. He's something in the pub trade down the Old Kent Road.'

My heart sank at that bit of information. The Old Kent Road is a bit like south London's answer to Dodge City before Wyatt Earp and his brothers moved in to clear it up. And the pubs there are a bit like the Last Chance Saloon, only with CD jukeboxes.

'What kind of something?' I asked.

He shrugged. 'Dunno. She was a bit vague. Runs one, owns

one, works in one. Whatever. But then that's your job, innit? Finding out.'

'I don't know,' I said. 'I'm getting a bit old for trolling around the Old Kent Road boozers. The average age of the punters has dropped to about fifteen down there.'

'But they still say you're the best.'

I'd love to meet this mythical 'they'. Perhaps they'd write me a reference so's I could get a nice, quiet, steady job with no stress and that fitted my personality. Like cleaning cars, maybe. 'I don't know,' I said again. 'I'm just looking for a quiet life.'

He changed tack then, and appealed to my better nature. 'If not for me, Mr Sharman, at least for Liam. He misses his mum something strong. Every night he asks for her, and I can hear him crying himself to sleep.'

At that I gave in. Next he'd be telling me about Liam's kitty-kat who had been off his milk since Sharon left. 'All right, Mr Miller, I'll try,' I said, putting up my hands in surrender. 'But I ain't cheap.'

He laughed, shook his head and reached into his pocket again. This time for a brown paper envelope. 'There's five grand there,' he said.

'That's a lot of dough,' I said back. I was feeling better already.

'Do you know how much interest I make on twelve million every week?'

I shook my head.

'Enough to pay for you for as long as it takes. Longer. If you need any more, let me know.'

'I will, but I can't guarantee anything,' I replied. 'A year's a long time. Even if I find her, she might not want to come back.'

'Tell her about the money. She was always fond of money, was Sharon.' Now we were getting down to the gritty bits.

'I'll do the best I can,' I said.

'Go for it then. My phone numbers are in there too. Home and mobile. Just call me when you find her.'

'All right, Mr Miller,' I said. 'Can I keep the photos?'

'Sure. I've got the originals.'

I gave him one of my cards. My office number was on the front and I scribbled my home number on the back. For five grand I thought he should be able to get in touch, even though I knew I'd probably regret it later. 'And I might want to speak to this Melanie,' I said. 'How do I get in touch with her?'

'Her number's in there too. All written down.'

'I'll get started then. I'll ring you if anything turns up,' I said.

'You will. And make it soon, please.'

After that there wasn't much more to say, so he got up and collected Liam and took him back through the rain to the car, which he neatly manoeuvred out of the space he'd found, made a three-point turn and headed back to Essex, leaving me with five thousand pounds, a bunch of photographs and the remains of his marriage.

It wasn't much, but I guess it would do for now.

There had been times when I'd been left with a lot less.

7

When he was out of sight I opened the envelope. Inside were five packets of brand-new fifty pound notes each containing a grand, plus a single sheet of paper with Ray Miller's two phone numbers. One a landline, the other a mobile. Under that was the name Melanie Wiltse, and a single telephone number. I folded the paper and put it in my pocket.

I just had time to catch the bank, so keeping a monkey back I locked up the office, walked down through the rain and deposited my new-found wealth and went home.

I was still living in the same poky studio flat not far from my office, although I'd had plans to sell up and maybe buy a little house in case Judith decided she wanted to live with me at some time in the future. That possibility was getting more remote by the day, but I still hoped it might happen.

I wanted to speak to her. Tell her about the job. Make her proud of me again. So at around four-thirty I phoned John Condie's home number in Aberdeen. His daughter answered. 'Susan,' I said. 'Hi. It's Nick Sharman. Is Judith there?'

'Sure,' she said in her cute Scottish accent and banged down the phone. I could hear the new Oasis album playing in the background. After a few seconds Judith came on. 'Dad?' She hesitated. 'Is everything all right?'

'Sure. I got a job.'

'That's good. What sort of job?'

'A missing wife.'

'Have you been paid?' Ever the pragmatist. Her mother's trait. Not mine.

'Yes. And very well paid at that. The geezer's just won the lottery.'

'You're joking.'

'Never been more serious in my life. You should see the car he's driving.'

'You and cars.'

'I know. Shallow.'

'You're all right.'

'Thanks. I just thought I'd let you know I've got gainful employment.'

'I'm pleased. I hope you find her. Now I'd better go. I've got revision.'

'Lucky you.'

We made our farewells and hung up. It hadn't been the warmest conversation I'd ever had with Judith, but then it hadn't been the coldest, so that was something.

I was feeling hungry by then so I nuked a Sainsbury's jacket potato with cheese in the microwave. I took it straight from the freezer so it was solid, and it took nearly five minutes to cook; even then the inside was still speckled with ice and the outside hot enough to bring up blisters on my tongue. Ah, the bachelor life. Don't you just envy us single citizens with no responsibilities?

When I'd finished my delicious snack, soaked in ketchup and eaten out of the plastic container it was cooked in with a wooden fork from the local chip shop, I celebrated my new job by breaking open a bottle of JD. I poured myself a drink and rang Melanie Wiltse's number. I got an answerphone, but no message. Just music. A lot of people seem to do that these days. Maybe it's angst, maybe it's to give callers a peek into their psyche, or maybe they're just too lazy or too embarrassed to speak. Melanie's machine gave me thirty seconds of 'Dancing Queen' by Abba. Work that one out for yourself. I left my name and home and office numbers and hung up.

After that I sat in front of the dead TV nursing my drink and decided to leave the mysterious Mr Grant and the lovely Sharon until the next day. What the hell, I was holding folding and decided to celebrate.

Round about eight I got dolled up in a suit, clean shirt, tie and freshly polished brogues and called a mini-cab. Whilst I was waiting the phone rang. A female voice asked if I was Nick Sharman. I agreed that I was. The voice, which had a slight east London intonation, told me she was Melanie Wiltse and said she'd got my message. She sounded puzzled and a bit suspicious.

'Do I know you?' she asked.

'No,' I replied. 'I'm a private enquiry agent. I'm looking for Sharon Miller.'

'Sharon. Why?'

'Her husband has hired me to find her.'

'*Ray*. You're joking, aren't you? The last time I saw Ray I was on my way to work and he was off to the housing benefit office. How could he afford to hire someone to find Sharon?'

'His circumstances have altered somewhat since then,' I told her.

'That's interesting,' she said.

'And he told me you might have some information about a bloke called Chris Grant.'

'That scumbag. I warned Sharon about him.'

'Did you? Listen, I wondered if we could meet. Where do you live?'

'Walthamstow.'

'Oh,' I said. Walthamstow is well off the beaten track.

'But I work in Blackfriars.'

'That would be more convenient. Are you doing anything for lunch tomorrow?'

'Nothing special.'

'Can we have lunch?'

'Who's paying?' she asked, a bit suspicious again.

'Ray Miller,' I replied.

'Blimey. Things must've changed. Yes, I'll have lunch with you, but it's got to be somewhere nice.'

'You choose,' I said.

'There's a decent place on Gabriel's Wharf. Do you know it?'

'I can find it.'

'It's called Gabriel's Brasserie. There's a bar next door called Studio Six. I'll meet you there at . . . What . . . ? Twelve-thirty?'

'Fine. How will I know you?'

'I'm blonde and I'll be wearing a mac. You're an enquiry agent. Make enquiries.'

I laughed. I liked that, and I hoped I'd like Melanie too. 'I'll find you,' I said. 'See you tomorrow at twelve-thirty.' And we both hung up.

A few minutes later my cab arrived and I directed the driver towards the West End. Of course he didn't know where the fuck he was going, but that's about par for the course. Eventually he managed to find Shaftesbury Avenue and he dropped me off *sans* tip. One day, one of those cabbies is going to invest in an *A–Z*.

I wandered the wet streets like a wraith looking for forgiveness. I dined alone in an expensive Italian restaurant on Dean Street and ended up in a chrome and acrylic bar close to Soho Square, full of women with bad skin, bad hair, bad clothes and bad marriages getting tanked up either on champagne or sticky, highly coloured drinks of a dubious nature and listening to Frank Sinatra on the in-house stereo. They were all looking for love, or some reasonable facsimile thereof.

I was all alone and I missed my dead wife and my daughter, but I wasn't seeking solace amongst the clientele. The thought of waking up next to a stranger again clenched my stomach like a vice. Love. No thanks. I'd had enough love for two lifetimes.

I got a stool at the end of the bar and settled in for a night of steady drinking and minding my own business.

On about my fourth Jack and Coke I suddenly had this strange feeling I was being watched.

I slowly scoped the room, and way back at a table in the far corner next to the Ladies was a young woman on her own. She looked to be about twenty, pretty, with long straight black hair and a floaty print dress. Every time I looked round at her she looked away from me. Now, I've been eyed up by women in bars before and it wasn't like that. There was no eye contact or smile. And she looked different from the rest of the punters. Like she didn't belong. When I turned away for the third time I just knew she was clocking me again and for some reason it began to make me feel nervous.

I had just ordered another drink and Dean Martin's greatest had come on the PA when I felt a tug on my sleeve. I turned and it was her. Close up, she was more than pretty. Beautiful even, with a nose ring in her left nostril and a lot of black on her eyes. She reminded me of girls I used to know back in the seventies when I was at university. Hippies. She even smelt of patchouli. A musky perfume I hadn't smelt for years. I felt like we were in a cone of silence when she spoke. 'Hello,' she said. 'I've been watching you.'

'I noticed,' I replied.

'No, no.' She waved a hand. 'Not like that. I'm sorry.'

'Don't be.'

'It's just that sometimes I get these feelings.'

'Don't we all?'

'You don't understand. I'm not hitting on you.'

'I'm flattered.' She didn't seem to get the note of irony in my voice. I thought perhaps she was too young for irony, but later I was to find out different.

'It's just . . . It's just that I see things,' she said.

'What kind of things?'

'All sorts. And it frightens me sometimes.'

Jesus, I thought. A fucking nutter. Just my luck. But I said nothing. Later, I was to find out that I was wrong about that too.

'I know it sounds weird,' she went on.

'I've heard weirder,' I said. 'Fancy a drink?'

'No. I've got to go. Please listen. I see that you are involved in something. Something dangerous. I see a bad moon rising. I see terrible things. A woman with a coffin and a skull. I'm not sure . . .' She hesitated. 'You're in danger. Maybe I shouldn't've . . .' She paused again. 'You don't believe me, do you?'

'I don't know,' I said.

'I'm sorry. I have to go. Just be careful.' And she turned and vanished into the growing throng.

'Wait,' I said, but she was gone, and when I hiked myself up on the bars of the stool to look over the heads of the crowd she'd disappeared. I stood up and pushed my way through the people, but there was no sign of her and I went back to my seat and ordered another drink.

8

I sat in the bar until it closed at three, then went and got a black cab home. I couldn't get the girl or what she'd said out of my mind. She was pretty, but a spooky little bitch. And she was right. I *was* getting involved with something. Something she'd warned me against, and although she might indeed have just been a harmless nutter, it kept preying on my mind. All that talk of coffins and skulls had got me jittery. And how the fuck did she know? I made a cup of tea when I got in and smoked a last cigarette before collapsing into bed around four. I dreamt about the girl in her floaty dress, telling me to beware. Telling me she saw a bad moon rising. Well, it wouldn't be the first.

When I woke up it was full daylight and it felt as if a couple of battalions of the Chinese army were doing a short-order parade ground drill inside my head. I moaned and checked my watch. It was already nearly eleven and I decided I was too old for staying up half the night. Or maybe it was something I ate. Depressing thought.

Eventually I crawled out of bed and under a shower, had a shave and got dressed. It was still raining which depressed me even more, especially as I had a lunch date with Melanie Wiltse when all I really wanted to do was to close the curtains and go back to my unmade bed and grab another few hours' sleep.

But, shored up with tea and toast, at eleven forty-five I called a cab and headed for Waterloo. At least this cabbie knew where the river was, which was something, and at twelve-fifteen precisely he dropped me off on the south side of Waterloo Bridge and vanished into the traffic in a blue haze of oily smoke and a swish of tyres on the wet road.

I walked along the embankment under the dripping trees to Gabriel's Wharf and found the bar that Melanie had described to me and ordered a beer. It was pre-lunch empty and there were no blondes *in situ*, with mackintoshes or without.

I lit a cigarette and waited. The bar had a view of the river which was the colour of old iron that perfectly matched the clouds that hovered over the city and leaked a soft drizzle that hardly dotted the puddles on the wharf. The place began to fill up as the lunchtime crowd arrived, shaking their umbrellas and wiping the damp from their hair. A blonde in a mac came bustling through the door, looked round and headed straight for me. 'Nick Sharman?' she queried.

I nodded and slid off my stool to greet her. 'How did you know?' I said as we shook hands.

'You fit the description. So he won the bloody lottery. That's amazing.'

My head still hurt and it took me a minute to catch up. 'Description? And how do you know about the lottery?' I asked. I was beginning to repeat myself.

'I phoned Ray last night after I spoke to you. Flattering though it is to be asked out to lunch by a handsome stranger, I just wanted to check your story. I was lucky to catch him at the old number. He's moving up market. And who can blame him with that sort of money? Mine's a G&T. A large one if he's paying. This bloody weather's messed up my hair.' She ran her fingers through her short, yellow, spiky locks that looked just fine to me.

'He is,' I said and called over the barman.

When we'd got our drinks we snagged the last free table in

the bar, and she said, 'I've got a long lunch. I want to know everything. He was a bit mysterious last night.'

'You still probably know more than me,' I replied, offering her a cigarette, which she accepted. She was a clone of Sharon. Good-looking, tall, shapely, and wearing a blue suit with a very short skirt. She wore a lot of jewellery. Rings and things, and a clunky gold charm bracelet on her right wrist.

'I doubt it,' she said. 'As I told Ray last night I haven't seen Sharon since she ran off with Chris Grant.'

'Ray tells me you know Grant.'

'I don't really *know* him. I've seen him with Sharon a few times, and the fewer the better.'

'Why's that?'

'He's a nasty bit of work.'

'How nasty?'

'It's hard to explain. I just didn't trust him. Too smooth.'

'And you don't like smooth men?'

'Not the kind water runs off.'

'But Sharon liked him.'

'Sharon liked what he could give her. If she'd known about the lottery—'

'She wouldn't have gone.'

'No.'

'So tell me about Sharon.'

'I thought this deal was for lunch.'

'It is.'

'Then let's go next door and get comfy.' The way she said it made me think she might have mistaken me for a lottery winner too.

We finished our drinks and went to the restaurant. I'd phoned a reservation through before I left home and our table was upstairs in a corner, out of the way, just like I'd asked for. Not that I'd known when I'd phoned that it had an upstairs, but, hey, I'm an enquiry agent. I made enquiries.

The table was by a window also overlooking the river, and straight away I ordered two more gin and tonics. Or is it gins and tonic? I can never remember. But I wanted Melanie in a chatty mood and I figured the mother's ruin would do the trick.

Whilst we were waiting for the drinks we scanned the menu and the wine list. If Melanie wanted to get comfy, who was I to argue? It was lottery money, after all. Better we should enjoy it than it got spent on lesbian fringe theatre. When the large Veras arrived we ordered: lobster for her and steak tartare for me. Plus a bottle each of the most expensive red and white wines on the list.

'You're spoiling me,' she said.

'Ray is,' I countered.

'Or you're trying to get me drunk.'

'Perish the thought.'

She looked up at me from under sooty lashes. 'I can handle it,' she said.

'Let's get back to Ray. How long have you known him?'

'Eight years, I guess,' she said, taking a swig of gin and leaving a perfect pink lipstick mark on her glass. 'Since he met Sharon.'

'And how long have you know her?'

'God . . . years. Twelve. Maybe more. Since we started clubbing it. I bumped into her in the Ladies at a club in Romford. "Borrow your perfume?" You know the sort of thing.'

I didn't, but I could imagine. Where I come from blokes don't do much perfume borrowing. It tends to get you strange looks in my local. Then I thought about Charlie. I'd thought about him a lot since our meeting in the bar, but I hadn't been in touch. Some friend. I put him out of my mind and nodded encouragement to Melanie.

'We started hanging out together,' she went on. 'Pulling blokes. You know the sort of thing.'

I nodded again.

'Then she met Ray. In the Hollywood. He had a few quid. And lots of medals from the army. She fell for him.' She wrinkled her nose.

'But you didn't,' I ventured.

'No. No. Ray's fine. If you like that sort of thing.'

'What sort of thing?'

'Someone who looks like Grant Mitchell from *EastEnders*. Mean and moody.'

'And you don't?' She didn't like smooth. She didn't like mean and moody. I wondered what the hell she did like and, more and more as we talked, whether I fitted the bill. It had been a while, and there was something about Melanie Wiltse that I quite fancied.

'I like men with more hair,' she said, and looked at my thatch.

'So *was* he?' I asked. I still had a job to do.

'What?'

'Mean and moody towards Sharon.'

'No. As it happens he wasn't. He was very good to her. Gave her everything she wanted. Too good really.'

'How come?'

'Letting her go back down the clubs after she had Liam. Letting her out on her own.'

'But she wasn't on her own. She was with you.'

'You know what I mean. She phoned me. Miserable as sin she was. Wanted a chum. I was up for it. I could use a chum myself.' The last few words hung over the table like a challenge.

'But not her new boyfriend.' Job. Remember?

'No thanks. I warned her about him.'

'So tell me. What does he do?'

'He said he ran a pub down the Old Kent Road.'

'But you didn't believe him.'

'I don't know if I believed him or not,' she said as our food and wine appeared. 'He had a flash motor.'

'What kind?'

'A Merc. A new one. Dark blue.'

'Very nice.'

'Sharon thought so. Ray was driving about in an Escort van.'

'Not any more.'

'I bet. How the hell did he do it?'

'Do what?'

'Win the bloody lottery. I spend a fiver a week and all I've won is a couple of tenners.'

'Just put down six numbers, I imagine. That's usually how it's done.'

'And he kept his name out of the papers. The other winner that week was some ex-footballer and the papers chased him all over the country. Ray just sat tight and cashed the cheque. We had a long chat last night.'

I just bet they had. 'I thought you said he was mysterious,' I said.

'Only about you.' I nodded as I sipped at my wine. It was very good. I could get used to it and it was helping my hangover no end.

'And you haven't seen Sharon since she left him,' I said.

'No. One day she was there, the next she wasn't. Ray came round but I couldn't help him. He was in a hell of a state, but then who wouldn't be? Skint and left with a kid to look after.'

'Did you expect Sharon just to dump them?'

'No, I didn't. She loved Liam, but she wasn't up to motherhood. Some women aren't. Me, for instance.' She pulled a face. 'Maybe if the money hadn't run out . . .' She paused. 'I remember once she said her mum was a better mum to Liam than she was. Maybe she just thought it was best for all concerned.'

I left it at that for a bit. 'So what do you do, Melanie?' I asked.

'I work for a foreign bank across the river in Blackfriars,' she said. 'Ludgate Circus. I number crunch on a computer. It's boring, but it pays the rent.' She looked down at herself. 'I have to dress like this for work, but at weekends I do what I want to do. Be what I want to be.'

'The dancing queen,' I said.

She grinned. 'That's right. But not as much as I used to. It's all kids now.' She must've been all of twenty-five. 'Spice Girls. You know.'

Having a daughter myself I did, and I nodded again.

As she pushed her fork into a piece of lobster her charm bracelet clanged on the edge of the plate and I looked at it. I blinked and shook my head at what I hadn't noticed before. She saw me looking. 'I've had it since I was twelve,' she explained. 'Birthdays and Christmas I get charms from the family.'

'Can I look?' I asked.

She shrugged and undid the clasp and passed it over. It was heavy, and amongst the pound note folded tight behind glass, and the tiny Routemaster bus, and the London cab, was a miniature coffin on the same link as a perfect little golden skull. The girl's warning from the previous night came back to me and my stomach lurched. 'Where did you get these two?' I asked.

'Sharon gave them to me. Years ago. On my twenty-first.'

'I guessed as much,' I said.

'Is something wrong?'

'No. How's the food?'

'Great.'

'Good.' But it wasn't really, and as I watched the rain outside got heavier, lightning danced across the rooftops opposite and thunder rolled down the river. I shivered and wished that I was anywhere else but where I was.

9

It all got a bit flat after that and she noticed. 'What's wrong?' she asked.

'Nothing,' I replied. 'I had a hard night last night.'

'I didn't, but I wish I had.' She smiled, and I knew we were getting into difficult territory.

By then we were into coffee and brandy. 'So you haven't seen Sharon for a year or so,' I continued.

'Not a sign.'

'And you haven't tried to find her.'

'I didn't think she wanted to be found. She cut all her ties to her family and friends and went off with Grant.'

'And you're sure you can't remember if he ever mentioned the name of the pub he's supposed to run. Or her.'

'We didn't have a lot of long conversations. We were having a good time. And the music was too loud.'

So that seemed to be that. 'Well, thanks for all your help anyway.' I gave her one of my cards. 'If anything comes to mind, give me a ring.'

'I'll do that.' She paused, and we might as well have been the only two people in the restaurant, and the rain spattered against the outside of the window. 'So what about you, Nick Sharman?' she asked.

'What about me?'

'Where do you fit into all this?'

'I'm the hired help. Just trying to earn a crust.'

'Is that right?'

I nodded.

'Where did Ray find you?'

'*Yellow Pages* for all I know. He said he had friends who'd heard of me.'

'And what does a girl have to do to hire you?'

'Be in trouble of some kind usually.'

'Say she's not in trouble but wants to get into some.'

I laughed, and almost blushed. 'Do you watch a lot of old films on TV?' I asked.

'How did you know that?'

'Just a hunch.'

'I love it when private eyes say that in movies.'

'So do I,' I said.

'But do you know what my favourite line of all time is?'

I shook my head.

She struck a pose. 'Tell me, Harry – do you know how to whistle? It's easy. You just pucker up your lips – and *blow*.'

'I might've guessed,' I said.

'Do you know what film that comes from?'

'Course I do.'

'What?'

'*To Have and Have Not*.'

'Well done.'

'Not very difficult. I've seen it on TV a hundred times.'

'What year then?' she demanded.

'Forty-five.'

'Right again. Bogart and Bacall.' She went all misty eyed. 'I love that film.'

'Me too.'

'So we've got something in common.'

'Looks like it.'

'Are you married?' she asked.

'You come right out with them, don't you?'

'It's the only way. Are you?'

'Not any more. I don't have a lot of luck with women.'

'Getting them, or keeping them?'

'Both lately.'

'Maybe your luck's changed.' She looked at her watch. 'Damn,' she said. 'It's getting late. I'd better get back. This has been great. Thank you.'

'Thank Ray.'

'I will.'

I called for the bill. It was hefty, but I paid up without a murmur and left a decent tip.

We got our coats and left. 'I'm sorry I couldn't have been more help,' she said as we stood together under the restaurant's awning looking at the rain. I thought of the coffin and the skull. 'You've been more of a help than you'll know,' I replied.

That seemed to cheer her up. 'Good,' she said. 'If you're ever in Walthamstow look me up.'

'I'll be sure to do that.'

'Thanks again for lunch,' she said, and she bobbed up and kissed me on the cheek. 'And say hello to Ray for me. And don't forget. Just pucker up your lips – and *blow*.'

We parted then and she headed for Blackfriars Bridge and more number crunching. I watched her departing back and the nice way her backside moved under her mackintosh and wondered what legitimate reason could get me to Walthamstow soon, before I headed for Waterloo and a cab home to do some thinking.

When I got to the flat I dumped my coat and poured myself a drink. I sat on the sofa and wondered about the girl who had spoken to me at the bar the previous evening.

There was only one way to find out, and that was to meet her again. I sat there for hours watching the rain running down the windows until it was time to call yet another cab and head for the West End.

That night I covered every bar in Soho searching for the girl in the floaty dress, but it was all for nothing.

I haunted the rain that went from hard to soft, from warm to cold, until my Burberry was soaked, but there was no sign of her.

Eventually, as midnight struck, I gave up my hopeless task and took a cab home to more dreams of floaty dresses and skulls and coffins that disturbed my restless sleep.

10

I woke up to a sunny morning that did little to brighten my mood. I'd had too much to drink again the previous day and felt like shit. I was beginning to prefer the rain. At least that suited my frame of mind.

I did the usual things you do in the morning and wondered if I shouldn't just call up Ray Miller and give the job the elbow. So far no harm had been done and all it would cost him was a couple of days' wages and lunch on Gabriel's Wharf.

Perhaps then I'd call up Melanie Wiltse and tell her she'd found the chum she was looking for.

But instead I decided to have a look down the Old Kent Road and maybe find Sharon working behind the bar of Chris Grant's pub and tell her she could leave those dishwashing blues behind and live a life of luxury on the proceeds of her old man's lottery win.

Oh, if only life could be that simple.

When I was dressed I called up another cab and headed towards the Elephant and Castle.

Now there are a lot of pubs on the Old Kent Road, and a lot more in the side streets off it, and I'm sure some of them are family-run establishments catering to a better class of customer. But most of them aren't. Most of them are huge barns of places frequented by south-east London hooligans looking to get pissed up, score as many illegal drugs as they can and pull a bird as quickly as is humanly possible. Even on a Thursday lunchtime the whole area had an air of gloomy menace that the bright sunshine couldn't dispel, and I wasn't particularly looking forward to my task as I entered the first boozer I came to.

But at least it sold lager, and as my throat felt as if it had been dry-wall cladded overnight I ordered the first pint of the morning and sunk half with one swallow.

My first interview pretty well set the pattern of the day. After I'd lit up a Silk Cut I called over the barman, a thick-set fellow in his mid-thirties who looked as if he'd rather be wielding a baseball bat against some recalcitrant punter than serving the dish of the day off the lunch menu chalked on the blackboard behind him. 'Is the boss in?' I asked.

'I'm the boss.'

'I'm looking for someone,' I said.

'Ain't we all.'

I grinned what I hoped was an honest-looking grin and said, 'True. His name's Chris Grant. I heard he ran a pub round this way.'

'Don't know him.'

'Or maybe he drinks in here.'

'Thousands of people do.'

'And he knocks about with this girl. Her name's Sharon.' I produced one of the photos Ray had left me. The barman hardly gave it a glance.

'Lots of birds named Sharon in here. Never seen her. Who are you?'

'My name's Sharman. I'm a private detective.'

He didn't look impressed. 'What you want them for?' he asked.

'Her husband's looking for her. Something to her advantage.'

'No mate. Don't know them. And I don't want you bothering my customers.'

At that hour his customers consisted of one man in a muffler and cloth cap and his dog, and a couple of suits with mobile phones who looked like they were slumming the lunchtime away from the city office.

'Fair enough,' I said. 'Just asking.'

'Well, ask somewhere else. We don't like coppers round here. Not public *or* private. Why don't you just drink up and piss off.'

So much for cockney hospitality, I thought, as I did just that and went on to the next pub.

I got variations on this conversation the entire length of the Old Kent Road, down one side and up the other, leaving a trail of my business cards to be kept, chucked or used as joint roaches from lunchtime through happy hour and on until almost midnight when I gave up, found a mini-cab office and headed home, my head still spinning from my hangover and my stomach sloshing with lager – and I wasn't one iota closer to finding my quarries than I had been that morning.

Or at least I didn't think I was.

11

I woke up late again the next morning with the remains of yesterday's hangover, or maybe the day before's, or maybe a new one, fuddling my head, a tongue the colour of old newspaper and a liver that ached like a bitch. This was no way to spend my life. I lay in bed until my bladder forced me up, and on the way to the bathroom I stuck on the kettle for a much needed caffeine fix. And still I was thinking about the girl in the bar and what she'd said. My thoughts were like a bluebottle trapped under a glass. They wouldn't stop buzzing around my head and banging on the edges of my consciousness. When I was dressed and on my third cup of coffee I sat on the sofa and planned my campaign.

As I hadn't been able to visit every boozer in the area on the previous day, I decided to go back to the Old Kent Road to continue my investigations. Now there's a word.

But this time I'd leave it until later and do an evening shift, it being Friday, which, as everybody knows, is the beginning of the week for the sort of south-London toe-rag I was looking for.

So that left the rest of the day to fill, which I did by doing my laundry and catching up on the daytime soaps.

In the middle of a rerun of *The Bill* on Sky the phone rang. I caught it on the third ring as the commercials began. 'Hello,' I said.

'Nick.' It was Charlie.

'Hello, mate,' I said. I heard an edge of insincerity in my voice and I hated myself for it.

'What's up?'
'Got a gig. Looking for a missing wife.'
'Same old same old then.'
'More or less.'
'Long time.'
'Been busy. You know how it is.'
'Yes. I know how it is.'
'How's business with you?' I asked.
'Same old same old. Shifting motors.'
We both paused.
'So what can I do for you?' I asked in the end.
'You know. Pay a bill. Be a friend.'
'I try,' I replied, but it sounded lame and we both knew it.
'Fancy a drink?' he asked.
'Sure. When?'
'Tonight?'
'Can't make it,' I lied. 'Got to see a man about a dog.'
'Fair enough. Another time then.'
'Yeah. Just give us a bit of notice.' I'd never said anything like that to Charlie before.
'I'll be sure to book.'
I felt like a shit. 'Sorry, mate,' I said.
'Yeah. Sure you are. I'll be in touch.' And he hung up.
I sat holding the receiver, looking at the pretty pictures on the screen, and justified my actions by thinking I couldn't do anything for Charlie's particular problems, but I knew I was lying as I gently put it back on its cradle.
As soon as I did the phone rang again and I picked up and said, 'Forget it. I'll cancel.'
'Sorry.' It was woman's voice. A young woman.
'Sorry,' I repeated. 'I thought you were someone else.'
'Obviously. Did you see her?'
'Who?'
'The woman with the coffin and the skull.'

I sat bolt upright, all thoughts of Sun Hill Nick, on the box, and Charlie forgotten. 'Who is this?' I asked.

'Don't you remember me?'

'Melanie. Is that you?' Although I knew it wasn't. It was a different accent.

'Was that her name?'

'You seem to know everything else. You tell me.'

'I don't know everything. Only some things. I told you that. *Did* you find the coffin and the skull?'

'Yes.'

'I thought you would.'

'Who are you?' But I knew. It was the spooky girl from the club. It had to be.

'You'll find out soon I think.'

It *was* her. 'I came looking for you the other night,' I said.

'I know. It wasn't the right time.'

'When is the right time?'

'I don't know. Maybe sooner, maybe later.'

'Are you taking the mickey?'

'No.'

'Then what?'

'I phoned to tell you to be careful. What you're doing is dangerous. But I know you won't listen. That's why I know we'll meet again, sometime soon.'

'Let's meet now. I can come to you.'

'No.' She was emphatic. 'Not today. Another time. When you need us most.'

'Us?'

She laughed. It was a good sound. 'You'll find out. I promise. Now there is something else.'

'What?'

'Dead flowers.'

'What?' I said again.

'Dead flowers. If you see dead flowers the time for us to

meet will be soon. But that is the time of greatest danger. When you see the dead flowers.'

She was beginning to freak me out. 'What do you mean?' I demanded.

'It will all be revealed.'

Jesus, it was like something from *Lord of the Rings*. Soon they'd be calling me Bilbo Baggins. Then I had a thought. 'How did you know where to find me?' I said.

'Haven't you been leaving your cards?'

'Yes.'

'There you are then. Please be careful. And your friend needs you.' She hung up on me.

I tried the recently installed 1471 to get the number she'd been calling from, but the call had been masked. I'd suspected it would.

I sat and mulled over what she'd said and I didn't like it. Not one little bit. Maybe it was my almost permanent hangover, or maybe it was something else, but I was feeling as jittery as hell.

And the thing she'd said about my friend. What the hell did that mean. I tried Charlie's office number but the answer-phone was on. His mobile was switched off and there was no answer from his home.

And to make it worse I realized that my ex-directory home number hadn't been on any of the cards I'd left the previous day.

12

I wasn't feeling much better, when, round about eight, I pulled my old leather jacket over the polo shirt and Levis I'd been wearing all day and called a cab again. It dropped me off in the same spot as the previous lunchtime.

There was a big difference in the atmosphere of the Old Kent Road that evening. It reminded me of a low-rent version of the main drag in Las Vegas, all neon lights and cars swishing along the tarmac. And the local faces were just starting to come out to play.

And some ugly faces they were too.

I lit a cigarette and started my search.

Miraculously it was still dry with a clear sky and as I went into the first boozer on my list I noticed the moon was coming up over the tower blocks that looked down on the main road to Kent.

A bloated yellow moon.

A bad moon rising. Things seemed to be going from bad to worse.

But I just shrugged and pushed open the door of the pub.

Jesus, but that was a night to remember.

By nine o'clock every drinker was jampacked to the doors, with the spillage standing around outside drinking and smoking and doing deals. There were girls younger than Judith, wearing hardly anything and already pissed and stoned, hanging on to the arms of tattooed Herberts with murder in their eyes. The soundtrack was Rave, Jungle, Techno, Trance or disco tracks from the seventies and eighties mixed with the roar of turbo-charged car engines, the screech of tyres and the ever-present scream from police sirens as car- and van-loads of Old Bill charged up and down the drag to break up the fights that kept erupting like volcanoes. Then there was the smell. Burnt onions and old grease from the kebab shops, spliff, fish and chips, cheap perfume and after-shave and the acrid odour of engine fumes.

Urban stink.

By ten I'd given up on trying to speak to any bar staff. They were too busy pulling pints and mixing cocktails behind bars awash with beer dregs. Instead I just pushed my way through the crowd on the off chance I might spot Sharon amidst the hundreds of other tarty-looking blondes enjoying their leisure. But looking for the proverbial needle in the proverbial haystack would've been easier. Not that there weren't plenty of needles to be found. They were lying around in toilets and crushed underfoot in the gutters off the main drag. Little silver implements of pleasure that with one scratch could kill the unwary with their residue of HIV and hepatitis.

Occasionally I showed Sharon's picture and screamed above the amplified music that I was looking for her, and I left another trail of my cards most of which got thrown on the ground and trampled under a parade of stiletto heels and Ben Sherman loafers.

But I've always been of the opinion that if you chuck enough shit up against the wall some of it will stick.

It was late-night opening that Friday and the pubs were licensed till three, but by midnight I'd had enough and I went into a cab office and got a ride home. When I got indoors I could still smell the detritus of the night on me, but I was too tired and drunk from the booze I'd had to buy as entry to the twenty or so pubs I'd visited to worry, so I just undressed, fell on the bed and was asleep before my head actually hit the pillow.

I didn't dream at all that night.

13

I was rudely awakened by a phone call at seven a.m. At first I thought it might be Charlie or the mysterious girl. But it was neither. It was Teddy, one of the controllers from the cab office two doors down from mine. 'Nick,' he said, 'someone's bricked your window.'

'What?' I said through the remains of my sleep.

'Your office window,' he said patiently. 'Someone's put a brick through it.'

'Oh shit,' was all I could think of to say.

'You coming down?'

'Fifteen minutes,' I replied, and put down the phone, got up, pulled on yesterday's smelly clothes and hit the pavement.

When I got to my office I saw that Teddy had been right. Where yesterday there'd been a plate-glass window covering the front of the shop premises I call my office, today there was a gaping hole and a floor covered in shards of glass. 'Shit,' I said again.

Before I opened up I went down to thank Teddy for calling. 'Sorry to be the bearer,' he said.

'Did you see anything?' I asked.

'Heard. But all the boys were out, and by the time I got out the door there was no one in sight. Kids, I expect.'

''Spect so,' I said. 'When was it?'

'Just now. I phoned straight away.'

'Cheers, man.'

'Anything missing?' he asked.

'I haven't had a look yet. But what's to steal? Last year's phone book?'

'I got the number of an emergency glazier,' said Teddy. 'Twenty-four-hour geezer. You insured?'

'The landlord is.'

'You better call the cops.'

'What are they going to do?'

'You'll need to report it to claim.'

'Shit,' I said for the third time. 'I'll be hanging around all day.'

He shrugged, I collected the number of the glazier and went and let myself in to my office, although I could just as easily have walked through the hole the brick had left.

I sat down behind my desk and reached for the phone to call Old Bill when I saw something lying at my feet.

It was a bunch of flowers done up in brightly coloured paper.

A bunch of dead flowers.

14

I sat with the phone in my hand and looked at the bunch of dead spring flowers in their gaudy wrapping; they seemed to look straight back at me. I had this really weird feeling, as I remembered what the girl in the bar had said to me on the phone the previous day, and I gently put the receiver back on its hook.

I gingerly picked up the flowers as if there might be a stick of dynamite attached, but all that happened was one or two brown petals fell to the floor. I looked for a note but there was nothing. What did I expect? Best wishes from a friend?

I sat holding the flowers for several minutes, then literally shook off the weird feeling and tossed the bundle into the garbage. Someone's idea of a joke. But not a very funny one. I had to locate the mysterious girl and find out if it was hers.

I lifted the phone again and called the local nick. The operator told me that someone would be round, but I knew I shouldn't hold my breath. Then I phoned the glazier and the receptionist there told me the same, so I settled down to wait.

First of all I checked to see what had gone missing, but like I'd told Teddy, there was nothing to steal, and it didn't look as if anything but the window had been disturbed. Then I found a dustpan and brush in the back room and set about clearing the glass, picking up the larger pieces and dumping them in a black garbage sack and sweeping the smaller pieces into the pan. I didn't really think I was interfering with evidence, and it was something to do. I put the brick that had done the damage on my desk.

Just as I was finishing the job I was amazed to find a uniformed constable on the doorstep. 'You were quick,' I said.

'I got the call when I was dealing with a domestic round the corner,' he said. 'Thought I'd pop in.'

'Nice of you to bother,' I said under my breath.

I explained who I was and what had happened and he made a few notes, but I could see he wasn't very interested and I couldn't blame him,

'Anything missing?' he asked.

I shook my head.

'This what did it?' He picked up the brick.

I nodded again.

'No forensic there,' he said. 'The surface is too old and rough.' As if I expected a SOC team to come charging round to take fingerprints.

'I thought that,' I said. 'Listen, I only reported it for the insurance. For my landlord, you know.'

The copper nodded and gave me an incident number and his number and said, 'I'll be honest. Nothing's going to happen with this. If someone had seen something . . . A description maybe . . . Probably just kids.'

I told him what Teddy had told me. 'I'll have a word with him,' he said. 'But to be honest Mr . . .' he checked his book, '. . . Sharman. I'd put it down to experience.'

'I already have,' I replied, and he left just as the glazier's van pulled up.

I didn't tell him about the flowers. What was the point?

The glazier, a young bloke in smart blue overalls, hopped out of his truck and came in to say hello before measuring up and putting a big sheet of hardboard over the window frame. 'Back tomorrow,' he said. 'Twelve o'clock suit you?'

'You work Sundays?' I said.

'We work every day, boss,' he replied. 'Make hay while the sun shines. Know what I mean?'

'I know what you mean,' I said.

'You pay me and claim back off your insurance, OK?'

I told him it was.

'Lot of this about,' he said. 'Kids, you know.'

I told him I did.

'OK, Mr Sharman, I'll see you tomorrow,' and he wished me a cheerful goodbye before hopping back into his van and driving off.

I always like to see a bloke happy in his work.

15

I went home and tried to watch TV, but my thoughts kept going back to the skull and the coffin, and the dead flowers that had been left at my office, and the girl who'd approached me in the bar to warn me about those very things. I felt paranoid and vulnerable. I knew it must have something to do with Ray Miller's missing wife. But what? I thought about calling him, but as I had nothing to report I didn't bother. I didn't think it was him who'd busted my window.

I tried Charlie again but got the same result as the day before.

About two the phone rang. It was Judith. 'I told you I'd ring,' she said.

'Glad you did.'

'I thought you might be out looking for your missing person.'

'Just taking a break.'

'I bet. Haven't you found her yet?'

'Not quite.'

'But you're close.'

'Someone thinks I am, I think.'

'What does that mean?'

'Nothing.'

Suddenly she was concerned. 'Are you in trouble again, Dad?'

'No.'

'Don't lie. I always know when you're lying.' Another trait she'd picked up from her mother. Laura had always known when I was lying too.

'Just some local disturbance.'

'Dad. Don't do this to me.'

I remembered her holding the smoking pistol after she'd shot the geezer who was about to shoot me the previous Christmas, and I cursed myself for giving her more grief. 'I'm sorry, honey,' I said. 'It's nothing really. A broken window. Kids.'

'It sounds like more than that to me.'

'I swear. It's nothing.'

'Oh Dad, why don't you stop all this nonsense and get a decent job?'

'I can't hold down a decent job,' I said wearily, probably for the thousandth time. 'And besides I'm too old to get back into the job market.'

She was silent for a moment that stretched like a piece of chewing-gum.

'You're all I've got left,' she said eventually. At least she didn't add 'For what you're worth'. Although I could hear the unspoken words. 'Don't you go too.' And she hung up without saying goodbye.

I put the phone down gently, poured myself a drink and thought about what she'd said, and realized the futility of trying to be someone you aren't and never can be.

16

A few minutes after I hung up the phone rang again. 'Hello,' I said.

'Nick.' It was a woman's voice I thought I recognized, but it seemed strange.

'Yes,' I said.

'It's Ginny,' and she sobbed a terrible sob down the line and I knew something was wrong. Badly wrong.

'Ginny. What's the matter?'

'It's Charlie. He's dead.'

'*What?*'

'He's dead.'

'Oh my God. What happened?'

'A car crash. Last night.'

'Where?'

'On the A3. On the way to Guildford.'

My head was spinning from the news. Not Charlie. Not old, dependable Charlie who I'd lied to yesterday about being busy when he'd obviously needed me. 'Why was he going to Guildford?' I asked.

'I don't know. He'd been going out alone a lot lately. Business.'

'Are you at home?'

'Yes.'

'I'll be round in ten minutes.'

I went out to the car and drove round to Charlie and Ginny's house. It wasn't far. Judith used to stay there when she came down to London. Charlie and Ginny had three girls themselves. One of Judith's age.

I stopped outside the house behind a marked police car and walked up the path. Carol, the sixteen-year-old, answered the door. She was crying and came straight into my arms. 'I'm so sorry, baby,' I said.

'Oh, Uncle Nick,' she sobbed. She'd always called me that. 'Why did it have to happen to Dad?'

'I don't know, sweetheart. I can't believe it either. Where's your mum?'

'In the front room with two policemen.'

I knocked on the door and entered as Carol went to the kitchen from where I could hear more crying. Ginny was sitting in an armchair. A uniformed constable was sitting on a straight-backed chair by the table taking notes and a uniformed sergeant was perched on the edge of one of the sofa cushions.

Ginny got up when I came in. Her face was white and stained with tears. I went straight to her and held her tightly.

The sergeant coughed. 'Sorry,' said Ginny, stepping back from me. 'This is Nick Sharman. An old friend of Charlie's. And the family,' she added.

The sergeant stood and shook hands. He was about forty and going grey at the temples. 'Good afternoon, Mr Sharman,' he said. 'I'm sorry we have to meet under these circumstances. My name is Boreham.'

'Good afternoon, Sergeant Boreham,' I said back. 'Me too. What happened?'

'To be honest we're not entirely sure, sir. There were no other vehicles involved. Mr Martin's car left the road and he sustained severe head injuries. We're not even sure what time it happened. The car wasn't found until first light. Unfortunately there was nothing anyone could do.'

'Jesus.'

'When did you last see Mr Martin, sir?'

'A couple of months ago. But I spoke to him on the phone yesterday. He wanted to see me but I had a business appointment. Then I found I could get out of it and I tried all his numbers but couldn't get through. I tried again earlier today, but there was no answer anywhere.'

'Mrs Martin was at the station with us,' he said. 'And the children were with a neighbour.'

'Of course,' I said, but my mind was elsewhere. What had Charlie wanted? As if I couldn't guess. And how had my refusing to see him helped him towards that fatal car crash on a lonely road near Guildford?

'Well, Mrs Martin,' said the sergeant, picking up his cap from the arm of the sofa, 'I think that will be all for now. We'll want to see you again, of course. But we'll be off and leave you with your friends and family. And once more may I say how sorry I am to be the bearer of such bad news.'

I saw the coppers out and followed them down the path and buttonholed the sergeant. 'So what do you think really happened?' I asked.

'Has he been having any kind of problems lately?'

'We've all got problems.'

'I know that. But anything you know about specifically. Business, personal?'

'Not that I know of,' I lied. As much for my own sake as for Charlie's.

'You say he spoke to you yesterday. Did he give any indications?'

I shook my head.

'Coincidence then?'

'I don't know.' And of course I didn't. But I had my own ideas. Charlie wants to see me. I snub Charlie. Charlie kills himself. Elementary, my dear Sharman.

'I'll be frank with you, Mr Sharman,' he said. 'It looks to me like he drove off the road on purpose. He had no seat belt on and there was an empty whisky bottle on the passenger side.'

'Suicide,' I said.

'I'm not the coroner. But I've been at this a lot of years, and I've seen some.'

'Yeah,' I said and watched as they got into the police car and drove off. We've all been at this a lot of years and seen some.

I went back into the house and Ginny had joined the three girls in the kitchen. There was a lot of crying and hugging and the kitchen roll was decimated. 'I don't know what to say,' I said to them.

'There's not a lot *to* say, Nick,' said Ginny.

I took her outside and back into the living room. 'Where's his body?' I asked.

'Guildford mortuary. They're doing a post mortem.'

'You might have to prepare yourself that he was drunk,' I told her.

'So what's new?'

'Like that, was it?'

She nodded.

'I'm sorry.'

'Everyone's sorry, Nick, but that won't pay the mortgage.'

'When do you think the funeral will be?'

'As soon as possible.'

'If you need anything . . .'

She took my hand. 'I know, Nick. You've been a good friend.'

But not as good as I should have been. 'I owe him some money—'

She laughed. 'Didn't you always? That used to make him laugh. You and your bill.'

'I'll pay it up to date.'

'I wouldn't worry. Charlie left a lot of insurance. I'll put the garage on the market.'

'You shouldn't think about that now.'

'Someone has to. There's the girls. Carol taking her GCSEs.'

'Judith too.'

'How is she?'

'Critical of her father.'

'That goes with the territory. Is she still up in Scotland?'

'For now.'

'Best place for her. Away from London.'

'I hope she comes back someday.'

'That's what I'll do.'

'What?'

'Move away from London. Get a place out of town as soon as Carol's taken her exams.'

'That's a good idea.'

She lapsed into silence and so did I. After a bit I said, 'Listen, I've got to go. But keep in close touch. If anything needs doing I'll do it.'

'I know you will, Nick.'

I kissed her on the cheek. 'Say goodbye to the girls for me,' I said.

'I will.'

'I'll see you soon.'

She nodded.

I drove home wondering how much I had to do with Charlie's death.

17

I got in and poured myself a large one over ice. I didn't know what to think about what had happened to Charlie. Didn't know and didn't want to know. Eventually evening came and I was starting to climb the walls, so I went out for a drink, but just as I reached the bottom of the street a bus came by heading for the West End and on an impulse I got on. It dropped me in the Aldwych and I walked through to Soho. I wanted to try to see the mysterious girl again and find out what she'd been talking about, and although I knew it was an almost impossible task, my feet led me through Covent Garden and into the wicked square mile of legend.

The place was packed with punters looking for a good time and I was pushed and jostled on the narrow streets.

I went to the bar where I'd first seen her but there was no sign, so I set off on another pub crawl, looking for another woman who might be able to give me some answers to questions I half didn't want answering.

It was no good and I knew it. I didn't know why I was wasting my time, but still something told me not to give up.

Eventually, as the boozers were chucking out, I ended up down at Gerry's club, a late-night haunt for actors, writers and musicians on Dean Street. It was just filling up with post-pub punters when I arrived. I found a seat at the bar, nodded hello to a few of the customers I knew and ordered a brandy and Coke from the barmaid. A black geezer was playing a mixture of jazz and cocktail-lounge music on the upright piano in the corner and I settled down for a quiet drink before heading home.

The stool where I was sitting gave me a good view of the room and the stairway leading down from the street, which was the only entrance, and I passed the time by clocking the comings and goings of the exotic clientele.

I sat there from eleven until twelve-thirty, and was just thinking about calling it a night when all of a sudden the girl I was looking for came down the stairs. Just like that, as if it was the most natural thing in the world. Which in a way I suppose it was.

I stopped with my glass halfway to my mouth. I couldn't believe it was her. After trying to find her for hours, it looked like she'd found me.

She was with another hippie-looking girl just like her, and when they shucked off the coats they were wearing I saw that they both had on similar, long chiffon dresses that clung to their bodies in a most attractive way.

They found seats at a table by the piano and my girl came up to the bar. She ordered some drinks and looked around, which was when she spotted me. She didn't seem in the least surprised, just smiled shyly and looked away. I caught the barmaid's eye and pointed to the pile of money in front of me and the drinks she was getting. She came over and I said, 'I'll get those.'

The barmaid shrugged, helped herself to some cash, and when she took the glasses to the girl she pointed in my direction. The girl smiled again, took one of the drinks to her companion, came back for the other one and walked round to where I was sitting. I budged up to give her room and she said, 'I knew you'd be here. Thanks for the drinks.'

'A pleasure,' I said. 'We didn't get introduced the other night. My name's Nick. But then you know that, don't you?'

She nodded.

'How do you know? And how did you get my home phone number? It wasn't on the cards I left.'

'Someone must have told me the other night.'

'I don't think so. No one knew me in that bar.'

'You'd be surprised what people know.'

I could tell I was getting nowhere fast, so I changed tack. 'So what's *your* name?' I asked.

'Matilda.'

'Nice name,' I said. 'Unusual.'

She wrinkled her nose. 'I hate it,' she said. 'Most people call me Matty.'

'Matty it is then,' I said. 'I've been looking for you.'

'I knew that too,' she replied. 'Do you want to come and sit down?'

'Why not,' I said back, and we pushed through the crowd to where the other young woman was waiting.

18

We sat down and Matty said, 'Nick, this is Madeleine. Madeleine, Nick.' Close up Madeleine was almost Matilda's double. Same hair, same eyes, same everything.

'Hello, Madeleine,' I said.

'People call me Maddie,' said Madeleine.

Then it clicked. 'Maddie and Matty,' I said. 'You two are sisters, right?'

'Twins,' said Matty.

'Interesting,' I said. Some detective, I thought. I *was* getting slow in my old age.

'Nick bought us these drinks,' said Matty.

'Thanks, Nick,' said Maddie, lifting her glass and toasting me. 'Cheers.'

'Cheers.' I touched her glass with mine.

'He's the one I was looking for,' said Matty.

'Lucky boy,' said Maddie.

'I don't know about that,' I said. 'And don't tell me, you knew I'd be here.'

She nodded.

'Of course you did,' I said and took a sip of my drink.

Matty looked serious and she shouted above the sound of the pianist playing 'Guantanamera', 'Did you do what I said?'

'What was that?' I asked.

'You know. Stop what you are doing.'

'No,' I said.

'What is it you do exactly?' asked Maddie.

I had wondered when one of them would. Or did they

already know? Probably. They seemed to know every other damn thing. But I answered anyway. 'I'm a private detective. I'm looking for someone. A missing person.'

'Who?' asked Maddie.

'A woman. Someone's wife.'

'Is she the woman with the coffin and the skull?' asked Matty.

'No.'

'But there is a woman like that, isn't there?' she asked.

I nodded. 'I told you that on the phone. She's a friend of the woman I'm looking for. I met her the other day. She was wearing a charm bracelet. They were charms.'

'And you liked her, didn't you?'

'She was OK.'

'Don't fib,' said Matty. 'You *did* like her, didn't you?'

'All right. I did like her.'

'She'd be good for you,' said Matty.

'How the hell do you know that?' I asked. 'You don't know her. Or me for that matter.' Even though she knew more than I'd given her credit for.

'Have you found this other woman yet?' asked Matty, not answering my question, though I was getting used to that. 'The one you're looking for.'

'No,' I said to her. 'But I think someone found me. By the way. What did you mean about the dead flowers.'

She paled. 'What dead flowers?'

'Come on,' I said. 'You told me to beware of dead flowers. On the telephone, remember? How did you know?'

'Know what?'

'About the dead flowers that were left in my office for me today.'

She took a long swallow of her drink and looked at her sister. 'Who left them?'

'I don't know,' I said. 'I thought you might.'

'Oh God,' she said.

'But what does it mean?'

'It means something really bad,' said Maddie.

'Like what?' I asked. 'It wasn't you, was it?' I asked Matty.

She shook her head and I believed her. I'd never really thought it was.

'Come on,' I pressed. 'What's all this about? Tell me.'

'You may not believe us,' said Maddie.

'Try me.'

'It's what we do.'

'What?'

'We foretell the future,' said Matty, as calmly as she might tell me she worked in the local chip shop.

'You're kidding,' I said. Although of course I knew she wasn't.

'No.'

'For a living? For a hobby? What?'

'Both,' said Maddie. 'And your future doesn't look rosy.'

'Are you putting me on?' I said.

Matty looked serious and licked her lips. 'No, Nick, we're not putting you on, believe me. When I saw you the other night your aura was flawed. I had to speak to you.'

'Well,' I said. 'I've been described in lots of ways in my life but never as a flawed aura.'

'Don't joke about it, Nick,' said Maddie. 'It really isn't funny.'

'And you thought I was getting into something bad,' I said to Matty.

'That's right.'

'But where did the dead flowers come into it?'

'I don't know,' she said. 'All I can tell you is what I see.'

'And a couple of days later somebody leaves me a bunch after smashing his way into my office. It's creepy.'

'So you are going to stop trying to find this woman?'

I shook my head. 'No. I've taken her husband's money. Anyway, I don't scare off that easily.'

'You'll regret it,' said Matty.

'I've regretted lots of things in my life,' I told her. 'This would be just one more.'

'Don't say you weren't warned.'

'I'd never say that,' I said.

'And your friend?' asked Matty.

In all the excitement and misery of the day I'd forgotten that she'd mentioned Charlie.

'Christ,' I said.

'Something bad happened, didn't it?'

I grabbed her hand. 'Who are you people?'

She tried to pull back but I wouldn't let her. 'Don't. You're hurting me,' she said.

'My friend is dead.' I eased off the pressure.

She looked at her sister. 'I'm so sorry,' she said. 'I saw something but I didn't know . . . What happened?'

'He died in a car crash last night.'

'Oh, Nick. What must you think of me?'

'I don't know what to think. Of you, of anything.'

'He was hurting, wasn't he?' she asked after a moment.

I nodded.

'Did he do it on purpose?'

'No one knows. Maybe no one ever will. Do you know?'

She shook her head. 'But he's at peace now.'

I shook my head back. 'Who knows?' I said. 'Who the hell knows?'

19

'Give me one good reason why I shouldn't just get up and get out of here,' I said after a long, silent minute which was only interrupted by the regular sounds of the bar and the pianist segueing into 'This Guy's In Love With You'.

The two young women looked at each other again and Matty said, 'No good reason. No good reason I can tell you now. But later maybe you'll regret it . . .'

'You're good, you know,' I commented. 'Frightening, but good.'

'We don't mean to frighten you,' said Maddie. 'You've either got the gift or you haven't.'

'And you've got it.'

'I think you know that.'

'I know something.'

'So are you leaving?' asked Matty.

'Shit no. I don't want to be alone tonight, and you're right, I might regret it later.'

'I told you you'd find us when you needed to,' said Matty.

'And you were right about that too.'

When we'd got another round of drinks in I said, 'So how *did* you two know I'd be here tonight?'

'You don't really believe us, Nick, do you?' said Matty. 'We told you, that's what we do.'

'But you don't know everything, do you?'

'Nobody knows everything,' said Maddie. 'Otherwise we'd win the lottery every week.'

'Like Mystic Meg doesn't.'

They both laughed, and the atmosphere seemed to lighten. 'Exactly,' said Matty.

'So tell me what else you see for me.'

'We usually charge.'

'I don't mind paying.'

'There's paying and then there's paying,' said Maddie, and I felt her knee against mine under the table.

'How old are you two?' I asked.

'Nineteen,' said Matty. 'I'm the oldest.'

'By ten minutes,' said Maddie. 'And she never lets me forget it.'

'So I have dibs,' said Matty. 'And don't you forget it, little sister.'

'I think we should take Nick home and read his fortune properly,' said Maddie.

And that was when I knew I was getting into some deep shit, but oddly enough I didn't mind in the least.

'Do you live together?' I asked.

They both nodded. 'And we've got some good stuff at home. Want to try some?' said Matty.

'What kind of good stuff?' I asked.

'Come along and find out,' said Maddie. 'It's not that far.'

'Fair enough,' I said. 'But I want to know what's in store for me.'

'Can't you guess?' said Maddie, and she finished her drink with one swallow, got up and started to put on her coat.

The girls lived in a loft apartment in Notting Hill Gate about twenty minutes drive away, and they sandwiched me between them in the back of a black cab that we caught on Shaftesbury Avenue.

We went down the Bayswater Road, did a right on Holland Park Avenue and into the maze of streets round Ladbroke Grove and finally pulled up outside an old factory right beside the Westway. Close enough to hear the sound of engines as cars raced along it.

'You live *here*?' I asked, when the cab had gone.

'Sure,' said Matty. 'Come and see.'

She unlocked a small door set in a pair of high wooden gates and led me into the courtyard of the factory where a pair of Suzuki Vitara soft-top jeeps with huge chrome wheels were parked, one red, one blue. 'Yours?' I asked.

'Presents from Daddy,' said Matty.

'Very nice,' I said.

We went round the side of the building, which seemed to be pretty dilapidated, and Matty rolled up a huge slatted metal door, opened the accordion door behind it and we were in a service lift. She pushed a button on the box that hung down from the ceiling and with a jolt the lift started upwards.

Their flat was on the top floor, a massive loft with high ceilings, black wood floors and raw brick walls that were draped with black velvet; a contrast to the desolate look of the outside of the place.

The furnishing was minimal, featuring lots of rugs and cushions, and as soon as we got inside Maddie ran around lighting enough candles to illuminate a cathedral, whilst Matty put a CD of seventies film themes on the stereo, got out a couple of bottles of red wine, poured out three glasses, sat cross-legged on the rug next to me and started rolling a very large joint.

'Before we start, Nick,' she said, as she licked the paper, 'I meant what I told you the other night. You're in danger if you don't stop what you doing. But then you're used to danger, aren't you?'

I nodded.

'And you won't stop, will you?'

I shook my head.

'Then we'll have to give you some magic to protect you.' She lit the joint, using a Zippo with her name engraved on the side. 'Maddie's got one too,' she said, and I wasn't in the least surprised. She inhaled deeply and blew out smoke, and I could smell skunk in the air along with the candle grease and the girls' musky perfume.

'Strong magic,' said Maddie. 'You like coke, don't you, Nick?'

I nodded again as Matty passed me the joint and Maddie produced a lacquered Chinese box from somewhere, opened it and took out a white wrap and a pill bottle. She undid the bottle and poured three tiny pills into her hand. She picked one up between her thumb and forefinger and held it out to me. 'Have one of these first,' she said.

'What is it?' I asked.

'Trust us. We won't hurt you.'

I believed her, more strongly than I've believed anything for a long time, so I took the pill, put the joint in an ashtray and picked up my glass. I put the pill on my tongue and washed it down with a mouthful of the rich, red liquid. Maddie and Mattie did the same with the other two tabs and Maddie started cutting out lines on the top of a mirrored-glass coffee table.

'So tell him, Matty,' she said.

20

Matty took my hand in hers and I felt a little jolt of electricity down my spine, although if there was any acid in the tab I'd been given it might've been that. Anyway, it wasn't unpleasant, and her hand was small and cool and pretty as mine rested in it. She smiled. 'Don't be frightened,' she said. 'Everything's going to be fine.'

'I hope so.'

Maddie kept on chopping, and the music kept on playing, and the skunk and booze and whatever was in the pill started to make my head spin. But not unpleasantly. Just like I liked, and I started to relax as the lights haloed slightly and when I half shut my eyes my vision started to strobe and I wanted to giggle at the effect.

'That's better,' said Mattie. Then she seemed to trance out. 'Oh, Nick,' she murmured. 'I can feel such sadness inside you.'

I wasn't going to argue with that.

'You poor man. You've lost so much in your life.'

'Tell me about it,' I said, and my tongue felt fat in my mouth. I licked my lips, then picked up my glass with my free hand and took a sip.

'The woman you're looking for is alive, but she's very unhappy. The man Ray Miller told you about is very bad.'

'How did you know his name was Ray Miller?'

'Trust me. I know. I see two other men. They are even worse. They want to hurt you. They sent you the dead flowers.'

'Who are they?' I asked.

'I don't know. I don't want to get close to them, their spirits are black. But you must get past them to complete your task.'

'Will I do it?'

'If your spirit is free.'

'It isn't.'

'I know, darling. We two shall free it. But you must trust us.'

'I do.'

'I know. I saw that the first time I saw you. And your heart is strong. Together the three of us will succeed. But you must want our help.'

'I do,' I said.

'Good.'

'What shall I do?' I asked.

'Nothing. We'll take care of you.'

'Why? Why me?'

'Because.' And that was all she said, and the word seemed to ring round the massive loft like a bell.

'No more now, sister,' said Maddie, and she reached over and touched Matty on her shoulder, which shocked her out of her trance and made her blink.

'Leave it for now, darling,' Maddie said to her. 'You'll tire yourself and the night is young. Nick, have a line,' and she held out a rolled-up banknote to me. 'There's all the time in the world.'

I took the note and slid across to the table and snorted one of the long, thick lines of cocaine Maddie had so carefully cut out on the mirrored top. It was pure and powerful and hit me like an express train out of control. 'Shit,' I said. 'But that's good.'

'And plenty more where that came from. Aren't you a lucky boy?'

'I think I am,' I said.

'Believe me you are. Lucky we found you. You don't even know the half of it yet, does he, Matty?'

'No,' said Matty. 'Shall we show him?'

'I think it's time.'

The music on the CD player had changed, lowered its tempo and got richer, but that might just have been the chemicals that were coursing through my veins by then.

'Sit back and enjoy it,' said Maddie. With one liquid move she was on her feet and she pulled her sister up next to her. 'Help me, sweetheart,' she said, and Matty fumbled with the fastening of her dress at the back of her neck. It slid down her body like water and pooled at her feet leaving her dressed in only a tiny pair of black underpants and a jewelled crystal that hung around her neck on a thin gold chain that caught the light and seemed to catch fire. Then, Maddie did the honours for her twin and the same thing happened; black pants and a flaming jewel, and they stood in front of me, almost naked, with the candlelight turning their bodies the colour of honey.

21

I watched them make love on a pile of cushions in front of me, writhing and sliding over each other like snakes. The room seemed to be moving gently like a ship at anchor, the candle flames sparkled, and I could almost see the music that floated gently from the speakers.

When I looked at my hand holding the glass of wine, every pore and hair stood out individually and through my skin I imagined I could make out the bones beneath the flesh. I'd been on psychedelic jags before in my life and I knew that whatever had been in the pill Maddie had given me was powerful stuff, but the worst thing to do, the stuff that bad trips were made of, was to fight it, so I just let it roll over me like the tide.

I kept watching as the girls, naked now except for the crystal pendants they both wore, seemed to my hallucinating brain to become one body, one being, giving each other pleasure. I wanted to join in, but when I tried, Maddie – or was it Matty – shook her head and said 'Wait,' and I could read the letters of the word as it slid off her tongue and broke on the floor like glass.

After what seemed like hours, when they were finished with each other, they came to me, and pulled me to my feet and took me further into the apartment to a bedroom that was lit by candles too, where a massive bed waited for us.

They undressed me and laid me down, and did things to me that I'd only imagined before, and I lost myself in their musky bodies, and they in mine.

I woke up with the sun crashing through the uncurtained windows and the candles gutted in their holders, the three of us entwined under the brightly coloured bed cover.

I lifted my head and I thought it was going to drop off. 'Shit,' I said, and tried to focus my eyes on my watch which was still on my wrist. It read eleven five. 'Shit,' I said again, as I remembered my noon appointment with the glazier.

I pushed the girls' limbs off mine, climbed off the bed, found my underwear and jeans, pulled them on and headed for the bathroom, trying to keep my face from sliding off my skull. I used someone's toothbrush and stuck my head under the cold tap until a semblance of reality returned. I towelled myself off, had a piss, then flattened my hair with my fingers and went back to the bedroom where I finished getting dressed.

I think it was Maddie who woke up first, but I was still somewhat confused. She stretched herself, wiped sleep from her eyes and said, 'Where are you going, lover?'

'I've got to fix a window,' I said, and it sounded stupid even as I said it.

'Forget that. Come back to bed.' She shook her sister whose eyes popped open, and said, 'Nick's going.'

Matty sat up, showing a lot of enticing body to me as she did so, and wailed. 'Nooo . . .'

'I hate to do this,' I said. 'But I've got an appointment at noon and I'm going to be late.'

'Wouldn't you rather spend the day with us?' said Matty.

'Of course. But I've got a job to do.'

Matty's face fell. 'You're still going to carry on?'

'I have to.'

'Will you come back later?'

'If I can. But I've got to talk to my friend's wife about the funeral arrangements and everything. I might have to spend some time there.'

'Of course you have,' said Matty.

I climbed on to the bed and gathered the two naked women in my arms. God, but it was hard to think about leaving. 'Listen, I have to go. I've got to find a cab.'

'Take one of the jeeps,' said Maddie. 'The keys are in the other room.'

'Are you sure?'

'Of course, the red keyring's for the red jeep, the blue one for the blue. There's a remote in each to open the gates. Just press the button on the right to open them, on the left to close them behind you.'

'Thanks,' I said. 'And thanks for a great night.'

'It was our pleasure,' they chorused as one, and both laughed.

I kissed them and made to go, but Matty grabbed me and took the crystal from around her neck and held it out to me. 'Wear this,' she said. 'For good luck.'

'What about you?' I said.

'Don't worry about me, I've got Maddie.' I took the proffered gift and slipped it over my head, and just for a second it seemed to burn my skin, but only for a second, and then it lay round my neck, cool and hard. They both kissed me again, and I left them to go back to sleep or whatever they got up to in that vast bed.

22

I found the two sets of car keys on top of a shelf in the main room of the apartment and helped myself to the blue set, then let myself out and took the elevator down. I opened up the blue jeep and slid on to the driver's seat. Inside the motor was a bit of a slum, but I had no time for finer things, and just hit the ignition. At least the engine sounded healthy, if something like a sewing machine, and there was half a tank of gas. Just like Maddie had said, there was a black plastic remote control on top of the dash with two buttons side by side. I touched the one on the right and the huge gates swung open. I put the little car into gear and pulled away. Once outside I dipped the clutch, held the car on the foot brake and closed the gates behind me before heading off. It was a bit like driving a mechanized roller skate, but I soon got used to it and sped across west London towards the river and home.

I got back to my office at twelve-fifteen and the glazier was just leaving. 'I thought you'd forgotten,' he said.

'Sorry, mate,' I replied. 'Something came up.'

'I can believe that,' he said back. 'You look a right mess.'

'Cheers. You got the glass?'

'On the wagon.'

'Well, get weaving. I haven't got all day.'

And then as I was fumbling with the door lock my phone started ringing inside. 'Shit,' I said, and pushing the door open I grabbed the instrument.

'Sharman,' I said.

'It's Ray Miller. Have you got anything for me?'

'Not yet,' I said, sliding into my seat behind the desk as the glazier started taking the wood off the window. 'But I'm working on it.'

'When do you think you will?'

'It's hard to tell, Mr Miller,' I replied. 'These things take time.'

'What have you been doing?'

'Asking around, scoping out the territory. Being warned off, I think.'

'Warned off? Who by?'

'I'm not sure yet. But as soon as people start to warn you off, you know you're on the right track.'

'So what's next?'

'More of the same. If I keep on asking questions, eventually I'll start to get the right answers.'

'I hope so.'

'So do I.'

'OK. I'll leave you to it.'

'You do that, Mr Miller.'

'Call me Ray.'

'OK, Ray. I'll be in touch as soon as something breaks.' And I put down the phone.

'Problems?' asked the glazier. He was turning into a regular pain in the arse.

'Nothing I can't handle,' I replied as the phone rang again.

'Popular,' said the glazier, as I lifted up the receiver. 'I see you work Sundays too.'

I ignored his remark. 'Sharman,' I said into the phone.

'You've been making yourself busy, Mr Sharman.' It was a voice I didn't recognize, croaky and deep, and just for a moment the crystal around my neck seemed to burn again.

'That's how I earn a crust,' I said.

'You got the flowers?'

I looked into the wastepaper basket where the bunch of dead flowers still lay.

'That's right,' I said.

'Take that as a warning then. Leave it alone.'

'Who are you?'

'That would be telling,' and whoever it was put down the phone.

I tried 1471 but the call had been masked.

'What do you do then?' asked the glazier, hammer in hand.

'Make myself unpopular. I'm not keeping you, am I?'

'No,' he said, and went back to work.

I phoned Charlie's home number. Ginny answered. 'How are you?' I asked.

'Just about as well as can be expected.'

'Lousy. Right?'

'You know, Nick, if anybody does.'

Sure I knew. I'd been there. 'I know,' I agreed. 'Have you made any arrangements for the funeral?'

'Yes. It's on Wednesday at West Norwood.'

'That quick?'

'I talked to the undertaker – sorry. They call themselves funeral directors these days, don't they – yesterday evening. He came round. I got a very nice coffin. Sorry. They call them caskets these days, don't they? The coroner agreed to release the body. There's going to be an inquest, but they don't need it. Charlie was pissed. Three times over the limit. Why did he do it, Nick?'

I could feel her pain over the phone. 'I don't know, Ginny,' I said. 'Do you want me to come round?'

'No. We'll be fine.'

'What time on Wednesday?'

'Two o'clock. We're not having a vicar, I couldn't bear it. Someone who'd never known Charlie spouting about what a great bloke he was—'

'He was,' I interrupted.

'I know he was, but something went wrong. Will you say something, Nick? He always thought of you as his best friend.'

'Of course I will,' I replied, but the words cut me like a knife and I could feel myself sweating under my arms. 'Are you sure you don't want me to come over?'

'No. You're fine, Nick. We'll see you at the chapel on Wednesday.'

'I'll be there,' I said, and we made our farewells and hung up. I felt physically sick at the way I'd let Charlie – good old dependable Charlie – down.

The glazier was still fiddling around with the wood. 'You going to be much longer?' I asked.

'About another hour.'

'I'm going for a drink then,' I said. 'If the phone rings, let it.'

23

But of course he didn't. As I was sitting in the boozer opposite having a cigarette and a medicinal lager, trying to clear my head of last night's excesses, and wondering who the hell was trying to warn me off, he came in. 'Phone call for you,' he said when he got to my table.

'I thought I told you to let it ring.'

'It wouldn't stop. Getting on my bloody nerves it was.'

'Who is it?'

'How do I know? Some bloke.'

I left my drink and followed him out of the pub, across the road and into my office where the receiver was lying on top of my desk. 'Hello,' I said when I picked it up.

'You took your time,' said another voice I didn't recognize. This one was high and nasal.

'I was out.'

'You Sharman.' It wasn't a question.

'Obviously.'

'You looking for Chris Grant.' Again a statement.

'Yes.'

'I know where he is.'

'How do you know I'm looking?'

'You left a paper trail up and down the Old Kent Road. I picked it up.'

'So where is he?'

'I ain't calling you for my health. How much?'

'How much what?'

'Don't fuck me about, Sharman. My time's valuable. How much will you pay for the information?'

'How do I know you're telling me the truth?'

'When I give you the place he's at and you find him you'll know.'

'Then I'll pay you when I find him.'

'Piss off! I want cash out front.'

'All right. You tell me. How much?'

'A monkey.'

'Five hundred quid! Are you going to come with me?'

'Piss off,' he said again. 'He's a mad fucker. You give me the dough and I vanish.'

'And I'm left with my thumb up my arse, five hundred quid poorer, at some old grannie's house who's never heard of him.'

'That's a chance you've got to take.'

He was right. 'OK,' I said. 'What's the deal?'

'We make a meet, you bring the dough, I tell you where he is and we part friends, never to see each other again.'

'Where?'

'There's a boozer off East Street. The Wise and Foolish Virgins. Know it?'

'No. But I dare say I can find it.'

'Be there at seven. Bring the money.'

'How will I find you?'

'Don't worry, I'll find you.'

'What's your name?'

'No names, Mr Sharman. Let's keep this anonymous. Seven o'clock,' and he hung up in my ear.

24

I put down the phone my end and went back to the pub. My drink was where I'd left it and I sat down and lit another cigarette. It tasted like cat fur. Interesting day. One of the most interesting for a while. First of all I get threatened and then I get the information I'm looking for. Coincidence or what?

I counted my money. Just over three hundred quid, so I took a walk down to the bank and got another deuce out of the hole in the wall. By this time it was almost one-thirty and my glazier friend was just finishing up as I got back to the office. 'How much?' I said. He told me and I winced. Still, the landlord would eventually pick up the tab, or at least I hoped he would.

'Take a cheque?' I asked.

'Cash or credit card only,' he said, so I dug out my Access and he whizzed it through a machine he had in the cab. All mod cons.

'See you again,' he said, when I'd signed the slip.

'I hope not,' I replied, and he smirked, got in his motor and drove off. But at least he'd made a decent job of the glass.

I called Judith then and told her what had happened to Charlie. She cried over the phone. They'd been close. He'd known her since the day she'd been born.

'Shall I come down for the funeral?' she asked.

'No,' I said. 'You stay where you are. You've got school.'

'I could miss a few days.'

I thought about the threatening phone call. 'No, Judith. I don't think it's a good idea.'

'OK, Dad, whatever you say. I'll send flowers.'

Jesus, I thought, flowers. Dead flowers. Could there be any connection?

Surely not. 'Good idea,' I said. 'The funeral's at West Norwood. One o'clock, Wednesday.'

'I'll be thinking of you. Send my love to Auntie Ginny and the girls.'

'I will.'

'And tell Carol we'll go out when I'm down next.'

'Sure.'

'I'm sorry, Dad.'

'Me too, darling.'

'Why does it always happen to us?'

'I don't know. I guess we were born under a bad sign.'

'You can say that again,' and she hung up.

I put the phone down and went home and had another think.

After an hour or so I decided I'd make the appointment with my mysterious caller and see what occurred.

At six-thirty I went back out to the jeep and pointed it north.

East Street market, or East Lane as it's known locally, was packing up when I arrived in Walworth. Another lot of suckers who worked Sundays. I steered the motor between the stalls and found a parking space and locked it up. There was a bunch of pubs dotted around for the market workers and I grabbed one geezer who was pushing a barrow and asked, 'Do you know the Wise and Foolish Virgins?'

'Blimey, it's been a while since I've met any bird what's a virgin round here.'

Cockernee humour. Don't you just love it? 'It's a pub,' I said.

He grinned. 'Yeah, I know it. Third road down on the left, say hello to Margie,' he said.

'Cheers pal.'

I followed the directions and found a small, flat-fronted boozer with flowers in hanging baskets outside, and a BEWARE OF THE DOG sign on the door. Below it was another sign that read: NO PUBLIC PHONE. NO PUBLIC TOILETS. Cockernee hospitality. I just love that too.

I arrived just after a nearby clock had struck seven times.

It was a neat little place inside, all polished brass and shiny mirrors, with three bar staff on. I went to the bar and ordered a pint from the blonde who was nearly as brassy as the ornamentation. Margie, I guessed. She served me and I scoped the bar. It was fairly busy with a lot of what I took to be market traders spending the day's profits. There was just one bar, a dart board, some tables and stools and a CD jukebox playing Eric Clapton at an acceptable volume. Nobody seemed to be taking any notice of me.

Then, out of nowhere, a little geezer popped up next to me. 'Sharman,' he said through the corner of his mouth, like the villain in a bad fifties British movie. But still I recognized the voice from the phone call.

I looked down at him and he looked up at me. 'Yeah,' I said. He resembled a sleazy little bookie's runner, with a greasy trilby, a tide mark of filth around the striped collar of his shirt, a tie with a knot the size of a pea, a check suit with a shine on the elbows and knees, dirt in his long fingernails, and a miasma of body odour and halitosis around his person. A real prince.

'Got my dough?' he demanded.

'Yeah.'

'Get us a goldie and come over.' And he scuttled across the carpet to a corner table that was almost private.

I ordered him a Scotch and carried it and the remains of

my pint to where he was sitting. 'Got a fag?' he asked, before I had a chance to sit.

I offered him a Silk Cut and he tore off the filter and lit the ragged end. A real connoisseur, I could tell.

'Chris Grant,' he said, when he'd taken a drag and swallowed half his drink. 'Why d'you want him?'

'That's none of your business,' I replied.

He sneered, showing nicotine-stained teeth. 'Don't get fucking clever with me,' he said.

'Listen, you little cunt,' I said back. 'Don't get clever with me either or I'll shake you till your eyeballs pop out. Now just tell me where he is or I'm off. I've got better things to do than sit smelling your armpits.'

'I know his mum,' said the geezer.

'Terrific. Happy families. What am I supposed to do with that information?'

'Nothing. But I also know where he lives.'

'So tell me.'

'So give me the dough.'

'If you're pissing me about pal . . .' I didn't finish the threat.

'I ain't.

I took the envelope I'd put the five hundred quid into out of my pocket and slid it across the table. He opened the flap and did a quick count. 'Satisfied?' I asked.

'It'll do.'

'So.'

He gave me an address on the Aylesbury Estate about a quarter of a mile from where we sat. I knew I could be easily mugged off, but it was all I had to go on, and besides Ray Miller was picking up the expenses, and with twelve million quid in his bin he'd hardly notice a monkey, more or less, so I said, 'Has he got a bird with him?'

'He's always got a bird somewhere.'

'This one?' I took out a photo of Sharon.

He gave it a glance and shrugged. 'Maybe. They all look the same to me.'

He was a big help. 'OK. Thanks,' I said. 'I hope I don't have to come back looking for you.'

'You won't,' he said, and he finished his drink and split.

25

I went back to the car and drove the short way to the estate, but not actually on to it. I didn't fancy finding the jeep stripped down to its bare body shell when I wanted to leave, so I parked up at the back of the Elephant tube station and went into the estate on foot.

The estate map was so defaced by graffiti that it was hard to figure out where the block I wanted was located, but after scratching at it for a few minutes I discovered it was about two minutes away, on the edge of the Old Kent Road. It was just like going home.

I walked through, and knew I'd been had before I even reached the block. In some vain attempt to restore the Aylesbury to its former glory, the local council was refurbishing parts of the estate, and the block I wanted was scaffolded up, covered in that weird green netting that builders use to stop stray chunks of masonry decapitating any passing citizenry, and looked empty. Windows had been stripped out and stared blindly down on me, and the whole place was dotted with piles of sand and odd bits of building machinery that the contractors figured were too big to be spirited away in the night by the local villains. At that time of the day and week it was deserted. At least some people had the weekend off.

Shit, I thought. Mugged off again. If I ever catch up with the little bastard who'd sold me this pup he'll be sorry.

But still I pressed on. Who knew? I might be lucky and find something.

There had been a half-hearted try at fencing off the block,

but most of it had been pushed flat either by the workers' trucks or chancers looking for something to rip off, and I climbed over and went looking for the flat I'd been told Chris Grant occupied.

It wasn't easy to find. Most of the front doors had been hauled off, but eventually I worked out it had to be on the third floor. Wearily I climbed the stairs until I came to the right landing. Of course the flat was empty, a mere shell waiting for refurbishment and redecoration. I stood on the walkway outside, in the chill wind that had sprung up from the east, and looked down at the cars heading into and out of town.

Five hundred nicker for this. I must be losing my touch, I thought.

And then from above me I heard a sound. Nothing much. Probably some old stray cat looking for a night's kip, but I looked up anyway, and the last thing I remember was seeing a huge chunk of scaffolding and its attendant planks of wood heading my way, and then nothing.

26

When I came to, the sun had sunk further in the heavens, it was twilight and I was hurting all over, with a headache more painful than the one I'd woken up with – was it only this morning? And worse, I knew I'd been suckered into a trap, and I wasn't sure if the trap had been totally sprung yet. Especially when I heard someone walking towards me along the landing and I couldn't shift the crap that was all over me.

Oh fuck, I thought, as I struggled with the scaffolding that was holding me down, they're coming to finish the job. After all I'd been through in my life, was this the way it was going to end? Cold stone dead on a fucking housing estate where you wouldn't want your dog to live, let alone die. Shit, I thought. This can't be happening.

And then, like a miracle, Maddie and Matty were leaning over me and brushing the dust from my face.

'What are you doing here?' I wheezed, as they gently moved the building materials off my body.

'We knew something was wrong,' said one of them, and I honestly didn't know which, I was having so much trouble keeping it together.

'How did you know where I was?'

'You were wearing the crystal,' said one of their voices as I lost consciousness again.

When I popped back to reality for the second time I could move, and although it still hurt like hell I could feel that no bones were broken. 'The car's downstairs,' said Matty, or at least I think it was Matty. 'We're going to take you home with us.'

I was about to tell them to take me to casualty, when I thought better of it. I'd rather be nursed by these two than some stern sister, and this way I wouldn't have to answer any awkward questions about where I'd been and what I'd been doing there.

And I knew they had drugs.

27

They got me up and helped me down the stairs and into the red jeep which was parked the other side of the broken fence. I slumped in the back seat and looked at the blood and filth on my clothes and realized I was lucky to be alive. 'You look a mess,' said Matty. Yes, I'm sure it was Matty. I was beginning to wake up.

'I feel like one,' I croaked.

'We'll soon have you feeling fine,' she said. 'Where's *my* car by the way?'

'Just round the corner,' I said, and managed to show them where before passing out once more.

I woke up when we got to Notting Hill. I was alone in the car with Maddie by then, but when I looked through the back window, Matty was driving the other jeep behind us.

The girls parked the motors and helped me to the elevator and into the apartment, where they undressed me again, but not in an erotic way this time. Then they helped me into the massive shower stall, undressed themselves, which I'm glad to say didn't leave me totally uninterested, turned on the water until it was pleasantly warm and joined me. They cleaned me up, then dried me gently, which made me even more interested, but they chose to ignore my condition, and took me to the bedroom where I dropped on to the bed like stone while they fetched plasters for my wounds.

'You want some morphine?' asked Matty, when they'd finished patching me up. 'It'll help with the pain.'

'Morphine,' I said. 'How the hell did you get morphine?'

'It's not difficult,' said Maddie. 'Didn't you know we were doctors?'

Shit, I swear those girls *were* doctors. 'Bring it on then,' I said, and they brought me two pills and a cup of some kind of herbal tea to wash it down. It smelt vile and tasted worse, and I begged for a Jack Daniel's or something similar, but they insisted, telling me it would make me feel better, and as I could hardly have felt worse, and I was in a weakened state, I drained it to the final drop. The last thing I remember was the pair of them, naked again, climbing into bed with me, one on either side, and the delicious warmth of their bodies as they lay next to me like the sisters of mercy they'd turned out to be. That's what I was going to call them from now on I thought, as I drifted off to sleep: the Sisters of Mercy, just like in the old Leonard Cohen song. And they were better than Tony Blair's new NHS by a long way.

28

I woke up with a full bladder feeling better than I deserved to. It was amazing. The girls were nowhere to be seen, and when I checked my watch, which miraculously was still working, it was past ten and the sun was bright outside. I found my pants and went to the bathroom for a piss. When I was finished I looked in the mirror and saw I had a lovely shiner on my left eye. I felt a bit stiff and there was some other bruising, but apart from that I was AOK. I went back to the bedroom, pulled on my dirty jeans and went looking for my saviours.

They were in the kitchen eating breakfast. 'How are you feeling?' asked Matty, when I went in.

'Better than I should. What was in that drink you gave me?'

'All sorts of things.'

'You should patent it.'

They both grinned. 'Want something to eat? Coffee?' asked Maddie.

I suddenly felt ravenous. 'Sure do,' I said. 'Have you got my shirt?'

'It's in the wash,' said Matty. 'I'll find you something to wear.' And she left the room whilst Maddie put some bread in the toaster. 'Scrambled eggs?' she asked.

'Please. Got any bacon?'

'We don't eat meat.'

There had to be a downer. Even in paradise. 'Fair enough,' I said.

'But I'll fry you some potatoes, and we've got mushrooms and tomatoes.'

'Terrific,' I said, and sat down at the table.

Matty came back from the airing cupboard with an oversized T-shirt that was soft and warm and fragrant, and I slipped it on.

Meanwhile Maddie rustled up a fast breakfast, which, even though it lacked one vital ingredient, smelt great, and I dug in as soon as she put the plate in front of me.

'Right,' I said when I was on my first cigarette and second cup of coffee, which I had a feeling was decaf but still tasted just fine, 'I've got a couple of questions for you girls.'

'Girls,' said Maddie. 'Isn't he sweet.'

'The spirit of chauvinism obviously isn't dead,' said Matty. 'Even though it was *girls* who saved his little life.' She put heavy emphasis on the word 'girls'.

'OK, OK,' I said. 'I'm sorry. And thank you. I mean it. If you hadn't come along Christ knows what would've happened to me. I'm eternally grateful, and that's no bollocks. But don't try and change the subject. Were you two following me?'

They shook their heads in unison.

'So how in God's name did you know where I was and what had happened?'

Matty shook her head in exasperation. 'We told you,' she said. 'You were wearing the crystal.'

I touched the stone that hung around my neck and shook *my* head in exasperation. 'And that told you I needed help?'

'We were there, weren't we?' said Maddie.

'I get the feeling that's all you're going to tell me,' I said.

They both grinned.

'So what are you going to do?' asked Matty.

'Find the little shit that set me up,' I replied. 'And whoever pushed half a building site on top of me.'

'Why don't you just forget it?' said Maddie. 'We can all have some fun together.'

I was sure we could. Convinced in fact, but I still had a job to do and I told them so.

Anyway, it was getting up close and personal. I don't like being ripped off and then left for dead.

I never have.

'Can I borrow one of your cars again?' I asked, when I'd finished eating and my offer to wash up had been refused.

'Sure,' said Matty, 'but be careful.'

'Don't worry about me,' I replied. 'I'll be just fine.'

But the looks on their faces told me they weren't convinced.

29

I collected the keys to the blue jeep again and, after kissing the girls chastely on their cheeks, hit the road back down south.

I got home and had another shower and peeled off the plasters they'd stuck on me. The cuts were dry, if still a little livid.

Not half as livid as I was. And getting more livid by the moment.

I got dressed in fresh clothes from the skin out, and wondered if I should get tooled up, but decided against it. I figured I could handle the sleazy little git I was looking for barehanded.

I went outside got back in the car and headed for Walworth again. I reckoned a little weasel like the one I was looking for would find an open-air market his natural habitat, and he wouldn't stray far.

I found a parking space and headed for the Wise and Foolish Virgins again. The pub was almost empty, with no sign of my nameless friend, but the same brassy blonde who'd served me before was still behind the jump giving an already clean glass a polish.

I ordered a half and when I'd had a sip I said to her, 'It's Margie, isn't it?'

She simpered and agreed it was.

'I was in here yesterday evening,' I said. 'I'm looking for the bloke I was with.'

She gave me a desultory shake of her platinum locks. 'Sorry.'

'Little geezer,' I explained. 'Trilby hat, suit. Scruffy.'

She shook her head again. 'Never mind.' I finished my drink in one long swallow, then with a cheerful 'Bye' I left.

I waited outside for half a minute then went back. The blonde was talking into the payphone on the bar and slammed down the receiver as soon as I entered.

'Nice try,' I said, found ten pence, put it in the slot and hit the redial button.

'Dog and Trumpet,' said a male voice after two rings. The Dog and Trumpet by great coincidence was a pub I'd passed maybe two minutes before I arrived at the Virgins.

'Cheers love,' I said as I put down the receiver, picked up the phone, ripped the wire out of its connection and slammed the entire thing down on to the floor, where the instrument split sending silver splashing across the carpet. I winked at the amazed barmaid and left, running as fast as my legs would carry me back the way I'd come.

I almost collided with Trilby Hat on the corner and he turned to flee, but I was too quick for him and grabbed him by the scruff of his grubby collar and ran him straight into the nearest brick wall, the force of the collision causing his nose to start bleeding.

'You and me gotta talk, shitface,' I said. 'Let me buy you a drink.'

I frogmarched him a hundred yards to yet another pub, pushed him through the door and up to the bar. 'Gimme a pint of lager,' I said to the barman, who didn't turn a hair at our entrance, 'and a large Scotch for my friend here.'

30

When we'd been served I propelled him to a seat in the corner. He was shaking so much he almost spilt his drink. I sat him down, sat opposite, but close, lit a cigarette and blew smoke in his face. 'You hurt my nose,' he said, mopping up the blood with his shirt cuff.

'Not half as much as I will if you don't tell me what I want to know.'

'What?'

'Who paid you to send me on that wild-goose chase last night?'

'I don't know what you're talking about.'

I slapped him round the face, but in a friendly way. 'Don't piss about, son,' I said. 'Or you're looking at a world of pain.'

He didn't like the word 'pain', I could tell. Who does? I certainly hadn't the previous evening. I heard the barman behind me cough, and I turned and made a placating gesture with my hands. He pulled a face but said nothing.

'I done a favour for a mate,' said the little weasel sitting across from me.

'Nice mates you've got. And I suppose he told you I wouldn't be around for a while. If ever?'

The weasel nodded.

'Name?' I said.

No response.

'It wouldn't be Chris Grant, by any chance? You'd better tell me or I'll break your fingers one by one.'

After a few seconds he gave me another nod.

'See. We're getting along fine. I think we could be friends. By the way, what's your name?'

No reply.

There was a folded brown envelope sticking out of the top pocket of his jacket and I plucked it out. He made an attempt to grab it back but I just knocked him on the nose again and he squealed and tears came to his eyes.

'Careful,' I said.

It was, as I'd thought, an unemployment benefit window-envelope and was addressed to Wallace Baker with an address in Kennington.

'Well, Wallace . . . Wally,' I said, 'now we're on first name terms you can tell me where I can *really* find Grant.'

Reluctantly he said, 'He part owns a pub in Albany Road called the Druid's Rest.' I hadn't got as far as going up Albany Road on my trips the previous week.

'You telling me the truth this time?' I said.

A third nod.

'You'd better be, Wally, or I'll make a home visit and, I promise you, you won't like that.'

'I *am* telling the truth.'

'I think I'd better go and see Mr Grant then.'

'He ain't in during the day much. He comes in later.'

'Now you wouldn't be lying to me, would you, Wally?' I asked. 'Again. Just to give Mr Grant plenty of time to line up a welcoming committee.'

He shook his head this time.

'Because if you are,' I said, 'and I come into any strife, some nasty men will make that home visit for me. Much nastier men than me, mate. And they owe me plenty. We're friends see, and they don't like their friend having the mickey taken. Get my drift?'

'I got friends too,' he said, summoning up a little spirit from somewhere.

'You told me. Chris Grant.'

'No. Other friends.' He was getting bolder by the second.

'The friends who were waiting for me on the Aylesbury, by any chance?'

''Sright.'

'So tell me about these friends of yours. One wouldn't happen to have a very gravelly voice by any chance?' I was thinking of my first mystery caller of the previous afternoon.

'Might 'ave,' said Wally.

He was holding his glass in his right hand on the table, and I leant over, took it in mine and began to squeeze. 'Tell me true, Wally,' I whispered, 'or else I'll huff and I'll puff and I'll break this glass in your hand and you'll be wanking southpaw for the next few weeks.'

He tried to pull away but it was no contest. I increased the pressure and fear flared in his eyes again. I smiled. 'All right, all right,' he said. 'I'll tell you, but I warn you, you won't like it.'

I eased off and he slopped the Scotch as he raised the glass to his lips.

'Another?' I asked.

He nodded. I caught the barman's eye, twirled a finger and he started pouring. 'Go on then,' I said to Wally.

'There's two of them,' he started to explain as the barman put the drinks on the counter.

'Hold on,' I said as I got up, paid for the drinks and bought them back to our table.

'Mr Freeze and Adult Baby Albert,' he continued, when I was seated again.

'Stop right there,' I said. 'Mr Freeze. What, like in *Batman*?'

'I dunno,' replied Wally. 'That's just his name.' Maybe he wasn't very big in comic culture. 'He's the geezer with the voice what sounds like his throat's been cut.'

'And the other one,' I said. 'What's his name?'

'He's a scary fucker,' said Wally, glancing round the bar. 'Fucking radio rental.'

'Adult what?' I said.

'Adult Baby Albert,' he said, as if it was a perfectly normal name. Well, part of it was at least.

'And what's *his* story?'

'He likes to dress up like a baby girl. A little frock and bootees and a nappy, and go to parties. Tea parties.'

I couldn't believe I was hearing this. '*Tea parties*,' I repeated.

'That's right. There's people put them on for people like him. That's how he gets his kicks. Blokes changing his nappies for him.'

I didn't want to think about it.

'And when he's not at tea parties eating jelly and ice-cream and shitting in his panties, he's out dropping scaffolding on people. Is that it?' I said.

'Or sticking knives in them, or shooting them,' Wally added.

I had to laugh.

'Don't,' said Wally. 'Don't laugh. Albert don't like people laughing at him. He's sensitive, see.'

'Sure he is,' I said.

'You better believe he is. He's got a bit of a weight problem like.'

'Amongst others obviously. I can't take this seriously.'

'You'd better,' said Wally. 'If you want to live to be much older.'

'And what's dead flowers mean in all this?' I said.

Wally nearly dropped his glass. 'Christ,' he said. 'You had some of those?'

I nodded.

'Then you *are* as good as dead, mate.'

'So why didn't they finish me off last night?'

'Fuck knows. Maybe they thought they had, or maybe they were disturbed. You just be thankful.'

'Oh, I am,' I said.

I suddenly had a thought. 'Do you know where Sharon Miller is? The girl in the picture I showed you. Maybe you could save me the trouble of meeting your friends altogether.'

'She could be anywhere,' he said.

'Is she with Grant?'

'Sort of.'

'What the fuck does that mean, Wally? She either is or she isn't.'

'No.'

'Spill it then. Come on.'

'The pub isn't his only business.'

'So.'

'He runs birds.'

'He does what?'

'He runs birds.'

It began to dawn on me. 'Like whores,' I said. Well it wasn't going to be budgerigars, was it?

Wally gave me a fifth nod.

'He's a pimp,' I said. I wanted to be sure.

Wally nodded again. You could have put the little cunt on the back parcel shelf of your car.

'But I thought Sharon was his girlfriend?'

'They all start like that. He pulls birds easy. He's a good-looking fella.'

Wally sounded jealous, and the way he looked himself I imagined that if he wanted female company it was quite possible he had to pay. Possible. It was probable. Definite maybe.

'And then?' I pressed him.

'And then he makes sure he's got something they need, and they have to do what he says to get it.'

'Something like . . .'

'With her it's smack.'

'Charming bloke.'

'You have to make a living.'

'And has he got Sharon strung out?'

'Probably.'

'And you don't know where she stays?'

'No idea. He's got places all over.'

'Lovely,' I said, and thought what Ray Miller would make of all this.

Wally shrugged, and the temptation to hit him again and keep on hitting him until he was the late Wallace Baker was overwhelming. 'The more I see you, Wally, the less I like you,' I said. 'Maybe you'd better get out of my sight before I decide that you deserve more than a bloody nose.'

'Is that it then?' he asked.

'That's it. But I think we'd both better forget that this conversation ever took place, don't you?'

Another nod.

'OK, Wally,' I said, folding the envelope and putting it the pocket of my jacket. 'That would seem to be all. For now. But don't forget what I've said. You haven't seen me today. *Capiche*?'

He nodded for a seventh time and wailed, 'You gonna keep my Giro?'

'That's right. For the address, you know.'

'But I'm skint.'

'Wally, Wally, Wally,' I said. 'What about the monkey I gave you last night?'

I copped his look. 'No, I haven't forgotten about that. I could reasonably ask for its return, don't you think?'

'It's gone. I owed a geezer.'

'I bet you're always owing geezers, aren't you, Wally? You look the type. But then I suppose you're earned it. If you've told me the truth this time.'

'I have. Honest.'

'I bet you don't know the meaning of the word. But that's by the by. And then there's the money Grant paid you.'

'I told you, I done him a favour.'

'Big on favours, are you, Wally? Sorry, mate, you'll have to report your Giro lost or stolen. But then, loath as I am to disbelieve a man of your demeanour, I reckon if you weren't holding, you'd've cashed this the moment the post office opened. So I think you'll make out. And if you don't – tough. I'm off now, Wal, and remember to keep well schtum about this little meet, otherwise something very bad will happen to you.' And abandoning the dregs of my pint I got up and left.

At the first telephone box I came to, I phoned directory and asked for the number of the Druid's Rest public house in Albany Road, and after a robotic voice told me, I dialled it. A male voice answered, almost inaudible against the sound of David Rose's version of 'The Stripper' in the background, so right away I got the ambience of the boozer.

'Chris Grant,' I said.

'Won't be in till after seven, try then,' and the phone went down hard.

Bad manners, I thought. Well, we'd soon see about all that.

31

I went home then and considered my options over a glass of JD on ice and a cigarette. I assumed Chris Grant knew what I looked like and had latched on to me when I'd been making enquiries up and down the Old Kent Road. Obviously one of the bar managers or staff I'd talked to knew him well and had told him I was looking. They were a close-knit lot round there. Then he'd got Wally to lure me up to the block of flats, and the two comic-book freaks Wally had told me about had tipped the scaffolding down on me. They obviously didn't care if I lived or died. Or maybe they thought I *had* died; or possibly the arrival of Matty and Maddie had scared them off. But from the way Wally had described them, a pair of young girls – sorry, young *women* – would've been just an appetizer. Maybe they had more powerful medicine than I realized.

But there was one thing Grant hadn't considered. By getting that rodent Wally to set me up, he'd also set himself up. Now I'd have to find out if Wally was more scared of Grant or me. I'd lay odds it was Grant, but then Wally might not want to tell him that he'd really grassed up his true location and the identity of his two murderous pals. And then there was his story about Sharon. That was a tough one, if Wally was to be believed, and there was no reason why he shouldn't be. So *that* was Grant's game. Find a young woman, spin her a tale. Wine her and dine her. Make her fall for him and promise her the world. Then get her hooked on one kind of narcotic or another and turn her out as a whore. It wouldn't be the first or last time something similar had been done. No wonder he could afford a new Mercedes.

But I felt so sorry for Ray and Liam and Sharon's mother. Which was why I couldn't tell any of them until I was sure.

I was looking forward to meeting Mr Grant. Not a great deal, but enough.

I was in a quandary, but then, when wasn't I?

I looked at my watch. It was nearly three, and this time I was going in armed. I remembered only too well looking up and seeing that scaffolding coming down. I could've been killed.

I went to my hidey-hole and dug out a highly illegal stubby .38 Colt revolver. Ten years it is now for owning a handgun, but I was prepared to take the risk. In fact there were more pistols around on the street than ever since the government banned them. Fuck me, Old Bill loved it. In came all those beautifully cared for revolvers and semi-automatics through the front door, and out they went through the back with the serial numbers filed off and a quick dip in a pan of paraffin to clean off any fingerprints. Then Mr Plod could afford a couple of weeks in Florida with the ever-loving and the dustbin lids on the profits, and who gave a fuck if a gun he'd supplied was used to bump off one of his colleagues back home? Just the luck of the draw.

I'd bought mine at the back of a block of flats in East Dulwich soon after the ban came into force. It was new, boxed and thick with grease, and it cost me three hundred and fifty quid. A bargain at twice the price.

I cleaned and loaded it with shiny new cartridges and stuck it down the waistband of my jeans, at the back, then drove down to my office to see if there was anything interesting in the post and to kill some time.

It was just the usual tax forms and junk mail, so I put the lot in the rubbish and sat back playing with a pencil, waiting for the evening to come.

And that bloody pencil saved my life. As I was tossing it into the air and catching it, I missed a catch, and as I bent to pick it up, the new window in front of me imploded, covering me with shards of glass, and something lethal thumped into the wall behind me.

I hit the floor, dragged out the .38, tried to get closer to the desk than a sausage to its skin, and waited for more incoming fire.

But there was none, and the next thing the door burst open and I heard Teddy's unmistakable voice shout, 'Nick! Nick! You all right?'

I put my gun away, stuck my head up from cover and replied. 'Not bad.'

'What happened, man?' he demanded.

I knew, but I wasn't telling. Someone had fired a single shot from a gun with a silencer, probably from a passing car, but all I said was, 'Just those damn kids again.'

32

It was the same copper and the same glazier. 'Someone doesn't like you too much, Mr Sharman,' said PC Plod.

'Looks that way,' I replied.

'What happened to your eye?'

'Walked into a door.'

'Careless.'

I nodded agreement.

'And the window was broken by the same method as the last time,' said the copper.

I nodded. I'd found a brick out in the desolation at the back of the building, left it on the floor and covered the bullet hole in the wall with a photo of Princess Di I'd torn out of a magazine. This was my fight, and I was getting angrier by the minute.

'Doesn't look like a brick did it to me,' said the mouthy glazier.

I gave him a tight-lipped smile.

'How do you mean?' asked Plod.

'The way the glass has shattered. I've seen glass broke in all kinds of ways, and this looks like something with a high velocity did it. Like a bullet.' He grinned then. Happy fucker.

The copper looked at me. 'Could it have been a bullet?' he asked.

'It was a brick,' I replied. 'And there it is. Dastardly, I agree. But a brick nevertheless.

'And you saw no one?' said the copper.

'I was thinking,' I said.

I could see he wanted to say more but he left it. 'Very well, here's another incident number, Mr Sharman. And if you do think of anything, get in touch with me at the station.'

'You'll be the first to know,' I replied, and with a frown he left.

'I'll block off the window again and get back tomorrow,' said the glazier. 'Or maybe I should just leave it. Looks like you don't have a lot of luck with glass.'

'I don't have a lot of luck with anything,' I retorted. 'But maybe that's about to change.'

33

After they'd left I sat at my desk pondering what had happened, and I wasn't happy about it. I hated being target practice for someone and I couldn't wait to see Chris Grant and communicate my unhappiness to him.

It was about then that I had a pair of visitors.

I didn't see them arrive because of the wood that covered the remains of my window, and the first indication I had of their presence was when the door to my office was rudely shoved open and they hustled into the building.

They were both big. Well over six foot tall. But one looked to be just as wide, and he had to turn almost sideways to get through the door. He came in first, dressed in a suit made from enough material to clothe a small army, and underneath the jacket he wore a pink shirt with some sort of weird appliqué around the collar. But it was his trousers that really got to me. They were massive, each leg wide enough to fit an elephant and with something underneath that I couldn't quite figure out. Like maybe he was wearing half a dozen pairs of underpants on top of each other. But before I could think too much about that his mate followed him in, and if I'd ever seen an uglier man it must've been in a nightmare. He had a face like something hewn out of the side of a quarry, and I've got to tell you these guys gave me the willies big time.

'Help you?' I asked.

'Sharman?' said the first geezer, in a voice that quavered around the contralto range and didn't sound like it should've emitted from a frame his size.

'That's my name, don't wear it out.'

'Funny bloke,' said Quarry Face, and his voice was exactly the opposite, seeming to reverberate like it came from the bowels of the earth. Despite myself, I shivered and felt for the reassuring weight of my pistol in the waistband of my pants. It was my mysterious caller from the previous day. Mr Freeze. Which made the other one Adult Baby Albert, and what he was wearing under his jacket was a little girl's dress in size XXXL, and under his trousers, a nappy. Simple. When you know what you're looking for.

Quarry Face closed the door and leant against it, darkening the room as he did so, and Fat Boy pulled up a chair and balanced one enormous bottom cheek on it. 'Had some trouble?' he asked, looking round.

'Not my week for plate glass,' I replied.

'You were lucky by the looks of it. You could've had a nasty accident.'

'You're not wrong.'

'We rarely are, as it happens.'

'So, who are you?' I asked and my hands were sweating. I just wanted to check.

"My name's Albert,' said Fat Boy. 'And my friend here is called Mr Freeze.'

I looked over at the other geezer. 'Like in *Batman* comics,' I said. I seemed to have had this conversation before.

'No,' said Albert. 'Like in if you don't start minding your own business you'll end up in a freezer down the morgue.'

'Now don't frighten me,' I said. 'I might shake right out of my shoes.'

'We heard you were stupid,' said Mr Freeze. 'But don't make a career out of it.'

'Are you two serious?' I asked. 'Or is music hall making a comeback.'

Albert looked over his shoulder at Freeze. 'Fucker *is* stupid,' he said. 'He gets dead flowers, he almost comes to a sticky end on a building site, he gets a friendly warning, then he gets a bullet through his window, and still he won't take the hint.'

'So it was you left the flowers,' I said. 'What was all that about?'

'Can't you guess?' said Albert. 'You get dead flowers, next thing you're dead. Simple. Especially for a man of your alleged mental calibre.'

'I thought you'd heard I was stupid,' I said. 'I'm getting confused.'

'We heard you were a bit of both,' said Albert. 'Now we've come here in a friendly way, and we've got other things to do today, so what we want you to do is forget you ever heard of Sharon Miller or Chris Grant or Freeze or me, and everything will be wonderful in your life. But if you don't, it won't just be half a block of flats falls on your head, it'll be the whole estate and you wouldn't like that, would you?'

'I wouldn't like that one bit,' I agreed.

'We've been good to you so far. Let you off easy. But that could all change. Will all change unless you get your nose out of other people's business.'

'I'm a nosy person.'

'We heard that too. But people have been known to alter habits of a lifetime. Take my advice and get into that mode. It'll be better for all concerned. You hear what I'm saying?'

'I hear you.'

'So there you go,' said Albert. 'Just chill out. Relax. Have fun. But stay away from our business and we won't bother you again. Now like I said we've got things to do. Stay here, mull over what we've said and I'm sure you'll come to the same conclusion that we have. Discretion *is* the better part of valour, you can take my word for that. Have a nice day, Mr Sharman,' and with a wheezy grunt he got to his feet.

'OK, Albert,' I said. 'But just tell me one thing before you go.'

'What's that?'

"Where the hell did you get that shirt?'

I saw Freeze pull a face.

'What's wrong with it?' said Albert quietly, and I could see I'd hit a nerve.

'Nothing, man,' I said. 'Pink's always been one of my favourite colours. I just wondered, that's all. It works for me, see, and I wondered where I could get something similar. Maybe in lilac or puce. But maybe a teensy-weensy size smaller.'

'You really are a funny man, Sharman,' said Albert. 'But the joke's over now. The next time I see you will be the last. Just make sure it doesn't ever happen. Get me?'

'Got you,' I said. The pair of them filed out of the room and Albert quietly closed the door behind him.

34

I sat there after they'd gone and considered the future. It looked like I had two choices; either do as they said or take a chance on the next bullet finding its mark. It really was no contest. I've always hated being threatened, and it always meant I was getting close. And anyway, now it was just me, me on my own. Everyone else was gone, and even if the next bullet *did* find its mark, I didn't reckon too many people would miss me.

But of course there was the other option. To swallow what had happened so far, put it down to experience and do what Albert had said: chill out, relax, have fun.

I thought I'd better have words with my principal.

I phoned the landline number he'd given me, but there was no answer. Then I tried the mobile. He answered on the fourth ring. 'Ray Miller.'

'Hello Ray, it's Nick Sharman.'

'You got some news for me?'

'Maybe. Maybe not. We need to talk.'

'So talk.'

'Face to face. It's a long story.'

'What are you doing now?'

'Not much. But I could find an errand or two to run if I wanted to.'

'Why not come over? We're just moving into our new place. You can help christen it.'

'I dunno,' I said.

'Come on, Nick. You want to talk, I want to listen. You can

meet Sharon's mum, Angela. There's a decent Thai restaurant in the village. It's in Egon Ronay. We can eat there or get food sent in. I want to show off the place. When you see Sharon I want you to tell her about it.'

'Yeah?'

'Yeah.'

'I really have got things to do.'

'And there's another reason,' he said.

'What?'

'You'll think this is daft. But you're the only person I trust these days. Apart from Angela and Liam. Everybody else I know just sees pound signs when they look at me.'

'Maybe I do too.'

'Everybody else would've been halfway here before I finished asking, looking for free booze and grub. You don't even sound keen.'

'It's a long drive to Essex.'

'Do me a favour and make it.'

For all his money he sounded desperately lonely and I softened. Like Albert had said: Chill out. Relax. Have fun. 'OK,' I said.

'I knew I could count on you. I've got spare trunks here, you can try out the pool. Or we can play snooker. Whatever you want. Stay the night. There's enough bedrooms to sleep a football team. You can have a decent drink. How does that sound?'

'Sounds good,' I replied. 'How do I get there?'

35

He told me which exit to take off the A12, and the route thereafter, which I scribbled down on the back of an envelope. I told him I'd see him as soon as I could, went out to the jeep and set off towards the river and then east to Essex. For once it wasn't raining. In fact it was a beautiful evening. I followed his instructions and eventually found myself in a pleasant little village that could have been a hundred miles away from London instead of the twenty or so it was.

Funnily enough, the journey took me close to Walthamstow, and I was tempted to drop in on a certain young lady and demonstrate my expertise at the art of whistling. But in the end I didn't.

I slowly drove through the village and along the main road beyond, looking for the turn-off he'd described, found it, and pulled up outside an imposing set of wrought-iron gates at just after eight-thirty. I hopped out of the car and rang the bell on an entryphone mounted on one of the brick gateposts. A woman's voice came over the speaker. I told her who I was, and the gates started to swing open. I got back in the jeep and drove up the long, gravelled drive, over a slight hill, and suddenly I was in a remake of *Dallas*.

Remember Southfork? This was it transplanted to south-east England. The sprawling brick ranch-style-built house with room for about forty cars to park out front, the patio complete with tables and chairs to enjoy eating breakfast whilst looking at the neatly tended garden, and the huge azure-blue pool to take a morning dip. Everything a lottery winner could want and more. Especially with the sun setting behind the pool and tinting the blue water with gold.

Parked outside the imposing front door were Ray's Aston Martin, a Bentley Continental and a Wrangler jeep with the top off.

I was almost salivating.

I parked my lesser jeep next to his, climbed out and headed for the door.

It was opened before I got there, and Ray, dressed in a pale blue polo shirt with a little crocodile appliquéd on the front, pressed chinos and deck shoes, came towards me. 'What do you think? ' he asked, looking round.

'I'm impressed,' I replied. 'Very impressed.'

He shook my hand and said, 'What happened to your eye?'

'Just a little local difficulty,' I said.

He nodded. 'Come on in. Meet Angela, say hello to Liam again and have a drink.'

I did as he asked and entered a vast hall with a polished wooden floor interrupted by brightly coloured rugs, white plastered walls and a high ceiling hung with a single, glittering chandelier. There were boxes and packing cases stacked everywhere.

'Excuse the mess,' he said. 'Moving. You know. But it'll be all right in a day or so.'

'No problem,' I replied.

He looked around again, every inch the proud home owner. 'Yeah,' he said. 'But it's lacking something.'

'How about a stuffed buffalo head on the wall? Then you could be in Texas.'

'Got one on order,' he replied, and I didn't know if he was joking or not.

'Ange and Liam are in the playroom,' he said. 'I thought I'd try and make him feel at home as soon as I could. This way.' And he took me off to the right into a massive room that was so full of expensive toys that it was like an annexe of Hamleys. Liam was sitting in the middle of the room on the floor surrounded by goodies and looking a little dazed at his good fortune. A woman was standing at the french windows, silhouetted by the sun, smoking a cigarette and holding an ashtray in her left hand. 'Ange, this is Nick Sharman,' he said. 'Nick, Angela. Liam. You remember your uncle Nick, don't you?'

The boy looked at me but showed no sign of recognition.

The woman moved away from the window and into focus. She was about fifty, blonde like her daughter, slim, wearing a short skirt and a white sweater.

'Hello, Nick,' she said as she put the ashtray on the top of a pile of boxes, transferred the cigarette to her left hand and walked towards me holding out her right to be shaken.

'Pleased to meet you,' I said, taking the proffered mitten and squeezing it gently. 'Nice place.'

'It will be,' she replied. 'When we're sorted and Sharon's home.'

I saw Ray shake his head slightly and look at Liam. Angela pulled an 'I'm sorry' face and took a drag on her cigarette. 'You found us all right then,' she said to me.

'No problem,' I said back.

'So where are we going to eat?' said Ray. 'You want to go out for Thai? Nick? Ange?'

'I don't mind,' I said.

'Can I have chips?' said a little voice. Liam had spoken for the first time since I'd met him.

Angela stubbed out her cigarette and knelt down beside him. 'Course you can, love,' she said. 'You can have what you want.'

She looked up at Ray. 'He can have chips, can't he?'

'Course he can.'

'I can make something here if you like,' she went on. 'Try out that flash cooker.'

Ray looked at me. 'Nick?'

'Whatever,' I said. 'I'm easy.'

'How about a good old fry-up?' said Sharon's mother. 'Egg, bacon, chips and beans?'

'Yes,' said Liam, suddenly looking a lot happier.

'Sounds good to me,' I said.

'That's it then,' said Ray.

'Go and have a drink and a talk,' said Angela to us, getting up and pulling Liam to his feet. 'Me and Liam will get it ready. I'll give you a shout.'

'Fine,' said Ray. 'Come on, Nick, the booze is in the other room. I made sure that was unpacked first.'

I smiled at Angela and Liam and followed Ray out to the hall again, straight across and into what I suppose was the living room, another huge expanse of wooden floor with a square hole in the middle, three sides being thickly upholstered sofas. A leisure pit I believe it's called. There was a pool table in one corner, a juke box in another, and a wet bar with stools in front ran along one wall. 'All the comforts of home. Go and sit down,' said Ray. 'What do you want to drink?'

'A beer.'

'Beck's? Bud? Heineken? Guinness? Bitter? What?'

'Lager. Whatever you've got.'

He went to the bar and came back with two bottles of Beck's and glasses.

'Mind if I smoke?' I asked.

'Sure. I'm going to.' And he opened a little drawer in the side of the sofa where he was sitting and took out a slim cigar. 'I'll get some ashtrays,' and went back to the bar for them.

When we were settled, he said, 'You wanted to talk.'

I nodded as I fired up a Silk Cut and said, 'This whole thing is starting to get complicated.'

'How?'

'Someone's tried to kill me twice, and today I had a visit from a pair of hitmen straight out of *Comic Cuts*. Only I don't think they think they're funny. That's how I got this.' I touched the bruise on my face. 'And that's not all.'

He leant forward and cigar smoke swirled up in front of his face. 'Tell me,' he said.

So I did. The only thing I didn't tell him was what Wally had told me about his missus being strung out and turning tricks. That could wait. For as long as possible as far as I was concerned. And I didn't tell him about the twins. I didn't want him to think I'd been taking bad acid on top of everything else.

'Well, you've certainly stirred up a wasp's nest,' he said, when I'd finished giving him the seven-inch version.

'And I was going to go in and stir it up more tonight at Grant's boozer. That was the errand I said I might run.'

'I'm glad you came here first,' he said.

'Well, I wasn't exactly relishing the thought. It was just something I had to do. Or maybe not do at all.'

'Were you ever in the services?' he asked suddenly.

'No. The police. My one time in uniform.'

'Yeah, I heard. You'd've made a good soldier, I think.'

'I doubt it. I don't take orders well. That was one of the reasons I'm no longer a copper.'

'The thin blue line, eh? And I was part of the thin red line. Brothers under the skin.' He slapped his leg. 'And all I got was a pay off, some useless medals and this.'

'At least you got paid off,' I said. 'I got shot and all I got was a bad foot and no pension.'

'Why's that?'

'I was a naughty boy.'

'How so?'

'Long story. Maybe another time.'

'Maybe. But if I'd not been shot maybe I'd've been a naughty boy in the Falklands.'

'What do you mean?'

He shook his head. 'Just stories. War stories about what our boys did.'

'Like?'

'Like they'd been watching too many Vietnam films. Shooting prisoners, taking souvenirs. Body parts, you know. Ears. Not good. I'm glad I came home.'

I nodded.

'And now you don't know whether or not to carry on working for me. Is that what you're saying?' he went on.

'It would be easier not to. Just to forget about the whole thing, return your money and take a long holiday.'

'Forget the money,' he said with a dismissive gesture. 'That doesn't matter. So what are you going to do?'

'I dunno,' I said.

At that point Angela came through and told us that dinner was ready.

36

We ate in the kitchen, which was the most comfortable room I'd been in so far. We sat at a big polished wooden table without a cloth next to a massive cast-iron range that looked to be a hundred years old. This was next to a very modern cube of work surfaces which incorporated a state-of-the-art oven, cooker and grill, a triple sink and an industrial-sized dishwasher. What looked like a thousand shiny cooking implements hung over the cube on stainless-steel racks. It was like the set for *Masterchef*.

Ray sat at the head of the table, Liam next to him, me at the foot and Angela next to me. She served up huge plates of egg, bacon, chips and beans. The adults washed the food down with chilled white wine, and Liam drank Coke. The food was good, the eggs over easy, and the chips big, brown and crisp. There was brown sauce, ketchup, salt and pepper and vinegar on the table. We didn't say a lot as we ate, because Liam's big blue eyes moved to each of us as we spoke.

When we were done Angela stacked the dishes in the dishwasher and said, 'You two men go and chat. I'll get Liam bathed and into bed.'

I expected ructions from the boy, but he just finished his Coke and added the glass to the machine.

'Say goodnight to Uncle Nick,' said Angela, and he surprised me by coming over to me, holding out his hand to be shaken and speaking only for the second time since I'd met him. 'Bring my mummy home please,' he said. 'I know you can.'

I held his small, soft hand in mine for a moment and swallowed. What could I do? 'OK Liam,' I replied. 'I'll do my best.'

'Do you promise?'

That was the killer. I hesitated, then said, 'I promise.'

He nodded sagely and Angela took his hand in hers and led him out of the room. I watched them go, and as she went through the door she turned and raised her eyebrows to me. 'I'll see you two when he's had his bath and I've tucked him in.'

Ray and I went back into the living room and he got a bottle of Rémy and three glasses, putting a decent-sized slug into two of them and passing one to me.

'Sorry about that,' he said. 'I didn't put him up to it. He may be just a nipper, but he understands what's going on. Poor little sod. He's so quiet sometimes, me and Ange forget he's there and say too much in front of him.'

'I understand,' I said.

'So?' said Ray.

'What can I tell you?' I replied. 'I always was a soft touch with kids.'

Ray smiled, and raised his glass in a toast and I touched mine to his with a clink.

'But there's something I have to take care of first.'

'What?'

'A personal matter. I have to speak at the funeral of a friend.'

'I'm sorry,' said Ray. 'A close friend?'

'Very. I feel bad about his death. Our families go back a long way. I have to be there. After what's happened I don't think I can go to Grant's until I've paid my respects. In case I don't come back. You understand?'

Ray nodded. 'When's the funeral?'

'Wednesday afternoon, three o'clock.'

'I don't suppose a couple of days is going to make any difference now.'

'I'm glad you see it that way.'

'I've lost friends too.'

After that we didn't say much.

Amgela joined us about half an hour later. 'He's off,' she said as she collected the glass of brandy Ray had poured for her. 'This bloody house, Ray. I'm not sure I'll ever get used to the size of it after my little place.' Then to me. 'You've got a daughter, haven't you?'

I agreed that I had.

'They're bloody murder, girls. I thought Sharon was sorted when she married Ray. How wrong I was. Are you anywhere near finding her?'

'I think I'm close,' I said.

'I don't know what happened to her,' she said wearily. Christ, she didn't know the half of it if what Wally had said was true.

'Leave it, Ange,' said Ray. 'Nick's heard it all before.'

'Maybe he has,' she said, and this time there was fire in her voice. 'But it doesn't hurt for him to hear it again.' I was beginning to like old Ange. 'She may be my daughter, but there's no excuse for her leaving you and Liam. You wait till I catch hold of her. Big as she is, I'll coat her properly.'

'I'll do my best,' I interrupted.

'I know you will, love. I heard what you said to Liam, and I believed you. He likes you. He told me when I put him to bed.'

'I'm flattered.'

She finished her drink. 'Ray. I'm knackered. I'm off to bed. Nick, I'll see you in the morning. Now don't you boys sit up all night drinking. We've got a lot to do tomorrow sorting this place out, Ray. I don't want you with a hangover.'

'All right, Ange,' he said weakly.

'Right. Goodnight then, both of you.' And she left.

'That woman,' said Ray when she was gone. 'I don't know what I'd've done without her.'

'She seems like a goodun,' I said.

'You can say that again. Want another drink, Nick?' He held up the Rémy bottle.

'Don't mind if I do,' I replied.

37

We finally got to bed about two-thirty, pretty drunk. We'd played a couple of games of pool, listened to a bunch of seventies 45s on the juke box, and I'd refused a swim.

Ray stuck me in a pleasant, if sparsely furnished room right at the back of the house. He apologized for the lack of amenities. 'Next time there'll be a proper guest room with en-suite,' he assured me. 'But I need to do some furniture shopping.'

'No problem, Ray,' I replied. 'I could sleep on nails.'

We shook hands and he left me to it. I found a bathroom down the hall and had a piss.

Next morning I was woken with a start by Liam shaking the side of my bed. I felt lousy. Hungover again, unshaven, and I'm sure my breath stank. He didn't seem to mind. In his hand he was clutching an Action Man dressed as a paratrooper.

'Hello, Liam,' I said. 'What time is it?'

He shrugged. Either he couldn't tell, couldn't care less, or time was immaterial. He held out the Action Man and said, 'For you.'

'What?' I said, still half asleep.

'It's my dad. For you.'

He dropped the figure on the bed and fled.

I got up and found my watch. It was just past eight. I located the bathroom again, did what I could to myself without the aid of razor or toothbrush, got dressed and went for a wander through the house, taking Action Man with me.

I found Angela in the kitchen. 'You look a bit rough,' she said.

'I feel it.'

'Have some tea. It's freshly made.'

'Sounds like a good plan. Ray pours a mean brandy.'

'I did tell you,' she said as she poured out a cup. 'He doesn't get many chances to let his hair down these days.'

'We just had a bit of a drink.'

'He needs a friend.' Then she noticed what I was carrying. 'What've got there?' she asked.

'Action Man,' I replied. 'Liam woke me up and gave it to me. Said it was like his dad.'

'In the pictures he's seen,' she said. 'I told you he liked you.'

'Will you give it back to him?' I asked.

'Not if he gave it to you,' she said. 'He'd be upset.'

'I don't want to nick his toys.'

'Blimey. Hasn't he got enough? You keep it, Nick.'

I put it on the table next to my cup. 'Where's Ray?' I asked.

'Gone down the village for the papers. He'll be back in a minute.'

And he was, as I was on my second cup of tea and the toasted bacon sandwich Angela had insisted on making me. 'A good night,' he said. 'We must do it again soon.'

I nodded agreement round my breakfast.

'So what are you going to do now?' he asked.

'What I told you. Go to the funeral tomorrow, and afterwards visit you know who. Sort this whole thing out, once and for all.'

'If you're sure.'

'A promise is a promise,' I said. 'I gave Liam my word. And he's given me this. For luck, I think.' I nudged Action Man.

'Then you're sorted, ain'tcha?' said Ray.

38

I might've been sorted, as Ray Miller put it, but I wasn't happy about what I was doing.

I had a sudden thought. 'Can I use your phone?'

'Sure. Use the one in the living room.'

I went through and from the paper Ray had given me I got Melanie Wiltse's number and rang her.

She answered quickly. 'Hello, Melanie,' I said. 'It's Nick Sharman.'

'Hello, Nick. You were lucky to catch me; I'm just off to work. What can I do for you?'

'I need to see you.'

'It doesn't sound like pleasure.'

'It would always be a pleasure to see you, Melanie.'

'Flatterer.'

'No. But this time it's about Sharon.'

'What about her?'

'Not on the phone.'

'When?'

'Now. As soon as possible.'

'But I told you I'm just off to work.'

'Can you take the day off? I'll buy you lunch.'

'Or Ray will.'

'No. This time I will.'

'That's an improvement.'

'So can you?'

'I suppose the financial world won't grind to a halt without me.'

'So you will.'

'OK, Nick. Where?'

'I'm up in Essex at Ray's. I have to pass through Walthamstow on my way back. Why don't I just call for you?'

'Sounds OK to me.'

She gave me her address and I put down the phone. I didn't know if I was going to see Melanie to help me with my search for Sharon. Or if I wanted to see her because I was attracted to her. Or if I was just killing time. I left soon after without seeing Liam again, but made Angela promise to let me know if he wanted his toy back. I stuck it on the dashboard of the jeep on the drive back to London.

With the help of my *A–Z* I found Melanie's street without too much trouble, and by quarter to eleven I was knocking on her flat door.

She opened it wearing a white T-shirt and blue jeans. 'I changed,' she said by way of a greeting. 'I took a day's holiday. They weren't pleased. I hope you're worth it.'

'Hello, Melanie,' I said. 'You look nice.'

'You're a bloody flatterer one minute, and all business the next,' she said, leading me through a tiny hall to a tiny front room with too much furniture and Sly & the Family Stone playing on the stereo.

'Good choice,' I said. 'I thought you'd be too young for sixties psychedelic soul.'

'You'd be amazed,' she said.

'Probably. I seem to spend my entire time being amazed these days.'

'So what can I do for you?' she asked for the second time that morning.

I looked at my watch. 'The pubs'll be open in a minute. Fancy a drink? Then we can go and eat. Is there anywhere decent round here?'

'What? Out in the sticks?'

'Not as sticky as where I've been.'

'Yeah. What were you doing in Essex? And you haven't shaved.'

'Sorry. I went to see Ray Miller at his new place. But why don't we talk about why I'm here over that drink?'

'OK,' she said. 'There's a bar with a restaurant in the high street. It's nothing to write home about. Burgers, you know? Do you think my figure can stand a burger and chips?'

'If yours can't, no one's can,' I replied.

'There's that flattery again. But I must say it's winning me over.'

She put on a short leather biker's jacket over her T-shirt and we walked to the high street which was only a few minutes away, and Beezer's Bar-B-Q and Rib restaurant was just opening its doors when we arrived. We sat at its replica Tex-Mex saloon counter and ordered a pair of Buds by the neck. I offered Melanie a cigarette and lit it for her and one for myself. 'This is probably not what you're used to,' she said, gesturing around the deserted bar.

'It serves booze,' I replied. 'And it's open.'

'Is that damning it with faint praise?' she asked.

'Not at all.'

'So what's Ray's place like?'

'Like this. But residential,' I replied.

She laughed. 'So what about Sharon?' she asked.

'Was she into dope?' I said.

'What kind?'

'Any kind?'

'She smoked a joint. Sometimes if we met some fellas with coke she'd take a snort. Why?'

'I've been hearing some bad things about her.'

'Like?'

'Like she's strung out on heroin and on the game to pay for it.'

Melanie stubbed out her cigarette in the Marlboro ashtray and took a drink.

'Bugger,' she said.

'But I also heard that Grant turned her on to the smack, and now he pimps for her.'

'That would be just the sort of thing I'd imagine he'd do. Have you told Ray?'

'No.'

'It would do his head in.'

'That's why I haven't told him. I want to find out for myself if it's true first.'

'Who told you?' she asked.

'A little geek who runs errands for Grant.'

'I assume he didn't volunteer the information out of the kindness of his heart.'

'No. I nearly broke his nose.'

She laughed again. 'Tough guy, huh?'

'I didn't have to be very tough to do it to this particular individual. But there are others in the equation who are more dangerous.'

'I've been meaning to ask you about the eye. I must say it gives you a certain rakish charm.'

'Now who's being a flatterer?'

'Did someone punch you?'

'No. Someone pushed a building over on to me.'

'Are you serious?'

'Never more so.'

'You don't live a quiet life, do you, Nick?'

'No. And it's getting noisier by the minute.'

39

She bought the next round, and we stayed chatting for another hour or so, but I could see her mind wasn't on the conversation.

'So what are you going to do next?' she asked eventually.

'Go to see Grant at his pub. Find out where Sharon is and try and get her away. But it won't be easy. Pimps seem to have a proprietorial attitude to their girls.'

'This is awful,' she said. 'I can hardly believe it.'

'Believe it,' I said. 'It's happening.'

We had lunch at the restaurant. It was a pretty basic menu. The burger was tough, the bun was stale and the chips were frozen, but the company was good and the beer came in bottles so no one could mess with the contents. I told Melanie about Charlie then, and realized that in fact he was the reason I'd called her. I needed to tell someone what had happened. Someone who didn't know him and really didn't know me either, and had no axe to grind in the matter. Melanie fitted the bill exactly.

'And you had no idea he was gay?' she said when I'd finished my story.

'No,' I replied. 'And I'd known him for two decades. Some detective, huh?'

'Not if he didn't want you to know,' she said. 'Some secrets get easier to keep as the years go by.'

'But he told me in the end. Then he wanted to see me the other night and I bottled out. Then he killed himself.'

'You don't know that.'

'I knew Charlie.'

'But not as well as you thought. You can't blame yourself, Nick.'

'But I should've seen him.'

'But you didn't. Don't beat yourself up about it.'

'That's easy for you to say.'

She covered my hand with hers. 'Not really. We're all guilty of letting our friends down, aren't we?'

'I thought that was what friends were for,' I said bitterly.

When we were finished I paid the bill and Melanie said, 'Want to come back to my place?'

'Sure,' I replied, and we walked back to her house and she got more beers from the kitchen.

'That was good,' she said as she sat next to me on the sofa. 'I enjoyed myself.'

'Me too,' I agreed.

'We should do it again.'

'I'd like that.'

'Nick.'

'What?'

'Do you want to go to bed with me?'

I looked into her eyes. 'Yes,' I said.

'Come on then.'

I shook my head. 'Not now. It's not right.'

'What's wrong with it?'

'Priorities.'

'And I'm not a priority. Is that what you mean?' She looked a bit miffed and I couldn't blame her.

'Exactly the opposite,' I explained. 'You are a priority, but I can't give you the attention you need. There's too much on my mind. Too much unfinished business. There's things I have to do and you'd get in the way.'

She looked back at me. 'Jesus,' she said, 'but you've got will power. I bet you could give up cigarettes.'

I shook my head. 'I'm addicted to cigarettes. I'm not addicted to you – yet.'

'I like you, Mr Detective.' She took my hand and squeezed it.

I squeezed hers back. 'I like you too, Melanie Wiltse.'

'So I'm going to have to let you go.'

'I need to find Sharon. She *is* your friend.'

'I wish she wasn't,' she said. 'Then I'd try and convince you to stay.'

'It wouldn't take much,' I said. 'Which is why I'm leaving.'

I kissed her on the side of the mouth and got up to go.

'You will call me,' she said.

'Of course. As soon as this is over.'

'Then make it bloody quick. You've made me wet, you bastard.'

'Hold on to that thought,' I said. 'I'll see myself out.' And with one more snatched kiss I left.

40

And all the way back to Tulse Hill I wished I'd stayed. I could've done. The funeral wasn't until the next afternoon. But somehow it felt disloyal to Charlie to go straight to the service from a strange woman's bed. As if I hadn't been disloyal enough.

I stopped by at my office and found a sniffy note from the glazier tacked to the door frame, saying he'd been, waited and gone. I pulled it off, screwed it up and chucked it in the gutter. If my only problems over the next few days were a couple of broken windows, then I'd be OK.

I stayed close to home for the rest of the day, watching TV and smoking too many cigarettes, and had an early night.

I dreamt about Charlie and Melanie and Adult Baby Albert and Ray and Liam and Matty and Maddie.

They weren't pleasant dreams.

The next morning I was up at the crack and dressed in my dark suit, white shirt and black tie far too early. I phoned the local florist and arranged to collect a spray of flowers, and sat looking out of the window for hours, tugging at my collar and trying not to spoil the crease in my pants.

Eventually the time came to leave and I drove down to the high street, picked up the bouquet and headed for the cemetery.

Of course it was raining. It had to be, didn't it, so I took my umbrella.

When I arrived there was already quite a crowd milling about around the entrance to the chapel beside the hearse and the pair of Daimler limousines that stood with their black paint slick with rain.

The congregation had mostly brought umbrellas too, and you could hear the rain drumming on the nylon like a saraband as I got out of the car and joined them.

Ginny was standing by the chapel door with the girls, welcoming the mourners, and I brushed through them to join her.

'Hello, Ginny,' I said, after I'd added my bouquet to the others lying on the grass, their cellophane already speckled with rain drops. I kissed her on both cheeks.

'Nick,' she said. 'Nice eye.'

'Hello, girls,' I said to the sad trio next to her, all three holding sodden white handkerchiefs in their black-gloved hands.

They all smiled sickly smiles at me but said nothing.

'Judith sends her love,' I went on. 'She wanted to come but I put her off.'

'She's seen enough funerals,' said Ginny.

'We all have,' I agreed, then I looked at Carol. 'She wants to see you soon,' I said.

'She phoned me,' said Carol with a sob in her voice. 'Last night. Wished me luck.'

'That's good,' I said. 'She loved Charlie.'

Carol started to cry properly at that.

'We're having a few drinks after at the Meadowlark,' said Ginny. 'Upstairs. It was Charlie's favourite pub. Will you come, Nick?'

'Of course,' I said. The way things were going with the people who were after me, it might be my last chance for a good drink.

'Sit at the front on the right,' she continued. 'You are going to say something.'

'Of course,' I said.

'Terry's going to start off.' Terry was Charlie's big brother. 'Then you, and that's it. I don't want this to go on any longer than needs be.'

'Right.' I touched her hand, smiled at the girls and went inside.

41

I hate funerals.

And I've been to some, let me tell you.

Too many.

I hate chapels of rest and coffins and wreaths and all the other paraphernalia. Every time I go into a church and see a box containing someone I knew up on the dais in front of the altar I get a terrible feeling in my gut, and today was no exception.

There was a lone figure in a navy blue suit standing in the middle of the aisle, facing the front. I walked up to him and he turned as he heard my footsteps. It was Charlie's brother. 'Hello, Tel,' I said.

'Hello, Nick,' he replied, taking my hand. 'Long time.'

'If we had to meet under these circumstances it could've been a lot longer,' I said.

'You're right,' and he sniffed hard.

'I'm so sorry,' I said.

'I know. You and him went back a long way.'

'Not as long as you two.'

'No. He was a little sod when we were kids. He drove me mad.'

'That what little brothers are for.'

'Course. You were one, weren't you?'

'That's right. At least he had you longer than I had my big brother.'

'Sorry, Nick.'

'No. Ancient history, Tel. We're here for you today, and Ginny and the girls, not me.'

'Right. Ginny wants it short and sweet. I'm going to say a bit, then you. Then we go out to the grave. Sod this rain.'

'It's a good day for a funeral,' I remarked. 'Miserable as buggery.'

'You're right. As we leave with the coffin they'll be playing some music.'

'Don't tell me. Rod Stewart,' I said. Charlie had always been a big fan.

Tel grinned. 'Had to be, didn't it? "Sailing" and "Mandolin Wind".'

As people started filing in, I propped my dripping umbrella in a corner and sat on the front pew at the side. Ginny and the girls and Charlie's widowed mother joined me. Charlie's mum sat next to me; she held my hand tight and I kissed her.

When we were all seated and the doors were closed against the weather, Tel stood at the lectern and said, 'We are here today to say goodbye to my brother and my good friend, Charlie Martin. We're not here to mourn his death as much as to celebrate his life and what he meant to our mum, his wife and his three lovely daughters. And of course to me, his big brother. We used to fight all the time when we were small.' He smiled. 'Hardly a day went by when Mum didn't have to separate us, and send one of us up to his room. I'll admit it was usually Charlie, because I was a better liar, and Mum would believe me when I said he started it.' Charlie's mum squeezed my hand as she suppressed a sob and I squeezed hers back. 'But after we lost Dad,' Terry continued, 'somehow none of that mattered any more, and the two of us promised that we'd never fight again, and we never did.'

I tuned out Terry's voice and wondered what they'd all say if they'd been sitting in that bar in Brixton earlier in the year and heard what Charlie had told me about what his life had brought him.

I came back as Terry finished. 'Charlie always looked on

Nick Sharman as someone he could count on, and Nick's here today to say a few words.'

Terry stepped off the lectern and I got up and took his place.

I looked at the sea of faces that filled the chapel; some I knew, some were strangers, and everything I'd thought of saying went out of my head.

'I don't know about you,' I said after a moment, 'but I had other plans for this afternoon.'

There was dead silence.

'And all I can think of is that this is the first time I've seen all of Charlie's friends together without a glass in their hands.'

A ripple of laughter ran across the room and I knew it was going to be all right. 'But I think we'll remedy that a bit later.'

Another ripple.

'What do you say about someone like Charlie?' I said. 'There's not enough words in the language. He was a husband, a father, a son, a brother. But to me, most of all, he was a friend. A friend for twenty years, who stood by me when a lot of others walked away.' Just like I'd walked away from him, I thought. 'He was always there. Twenty-four hours a day, though he moaned and groaned about it. But I always knew I could count on him. I could count on him for money. I could count on him for a sympathetic ear, and I could count on him to come out in the middle of the night with a tow truck and get me home when one of the motors he'd lumbered me with gave up the ghost.' A louder ripple of laughter, and even Ginny smiled at that one, because it was usually her who answered the phone. 'But it wasn't only Charlie,' I went on, looking at the front row of the pews where Terry had rejoined the family. 'It was Ginny and the girls too. And before them Charlie's mum and dad and Terry. I've known the Martins for longer than I like to remember, and I've never had anything but a warm welcome from any of them, even though

I was often being a nuisance, and if they'd had any sense they'd've shut the door in my face. I've had some bad times over the years and Charlie was always the first to rally round and the last to leave. Sadly, he's left us now, far too soon, and I'm going to miss him. But I know I won't be the only one. I look at your faces and I can see that as long as we all shall live, so will Charlie. And I can't think of any finer memorial than that.'

I stood down then and walked back to my seat and Tel must've made some sort of signal because the doors of the chapel opened, the undertaker's men came in, and everyone stood as the sound of Rod Stewart's voice filled the building and the service was all over.

42

We stood in the rain as they lowered Charlie's body into the ground, and his mum held one of my arms and Carol held the other; Tel had his arm round Ginny and the other two girls. The rain blew under my umbrella and I was glad as the raindrops on my face disguised my tears.

When the JCB with the shovel attachment moved in to fill the hole, the congregation slogged back up the hill through the grey curtain of rain to the cars and we drove in convoy to the Meadowlark in Dulwich Village.

I hate wakes as well, and I've been to some of those too, but at least you get to have a drink.

Upstairs at the Meadowlark was exactly as you'd imagine a south London boozer to be. A high, embossed ceiling, red flock wallpaper, chairs round the walls, a few scattered tables, a small bar in one corner and a tiny stage opposite. It was cold and damp inside and our wet clothes soon steamed up the windows.

Ginny and Tel and Tel's mum and the girls sat at one table, and the guests circled round them, passing on their commiserations one by one. I made straight for the bar and ordered a large brandy. The family had put a few hundred quid behind the bar but I insisted on paying. When I'd got my drink I found a spare chair, rubbed condensation off the window pane next to it, lit a Silk Cut, and stared down at the street below.

'Penny for 'em,' said a man's voice when I was about halfway through the cigarette and the drink.

I looked up. It was a bloke called Malcolm something-or-other who used to wholesale cars to Charlie. Mostly reps' cars, nearly new but high mileage. I'd never been keen on him, but I'd bumped into him a few times with Charlie in various pubs round about.

'Hello, Malcolm,' I said.

'Bad do,' he remarked. 'Charlie was a good customer.'

'You'll survive.'

'Ginny's packing the business in. There's a bargain there waiting for someone.'

'Why not make an offer?' I said.

'Not me, Nick. I like to move around. Can't be tied down. Nice things you said about him.'

'And true,' I said.

'That's bloody right, Nick,' another voice interrupted. 'Bloody right.' This time I smiled. The owner was someone I'd known nearly as long as Charlie himself. Paul Betteridge. A one-time petty thief who'd discovered a talent for art in the shovel, and now made a fair living flogging canvases to debutantes and trustafarians who thought it was too, too cool to be seen buying from a convicted felon, even if he hadn't done time since the seventies. 'How's the boy?' he asked in an accent that was several classes more up-market than when I'd first met him.

'Good,' I said. 'Apart from all this. How are you?'

'Can't complain.' And indeed it appeared that he couldn't, judging by the expensive look of the fabric of the black suit he was wearing.

'I can see that,' I said. 'You hanging round Groucho's again?'

'No. Groucho's is a wee bit passé. Soho House now.'

'Excuse *me*,' I said.

'Well, you south Londoners never had any style.'

'And you'd know.'

'Terrible thing about Charlie,' he said, taking a seat next to me. 'He was one of the best.'

'I know,' I said.

In time we were joined by one or two other mutual friends and the booze kept on coming and the room warmed up and we all dried off.

'He thought the world of you, Nick,' said Big John Fowler, a pro wrestler turned greengrocer, who came over with a tray loaded down with bottles of lager.

'The feeling was mutual,' I replied, taking one and juggling my brandy with the other hand. 'I just wish I'd paid him the money I owed him.'

'He loved all that,' interjected Bobby Lander, who ran a wholesale tyre business just down the road from Charlie's lot.

'Yes,' said Paul. 'It was the frisson of danger you added to his mundane life.'

'He thought you were the boy,' said Big John. 'Always full of stories about what you'd been up to.'

'No,' I said. 'I wasn't the boy. I was the prat. Charlie was the one who kept a business and his family together. Look at the mess I've made of my marriages. He was the boy if anyone was.'

'Maybe he fancied you,' said Malcolm, now halfway pissed and getting a bit too loud.

'Shut up,' said Big John, and he flexed his massive shoulders. 'This ain't no time for your stupid jokes.' And Malcolm did as he was told.

And then it struck me. Maybe Charlie had fancied me. And that was the worst thought I'd had of all.

43

The wake went on till closing time.

I got a cab home and collapsed into bed where I slept until noon the next day. I got shaved, showered and dressed and took a walk through to Dulwich to collect my car. At seven that evening I drove to Albany Road, found the Druid's Rest pub and parked round the corner.

I walked in at seven-thirty exactly and the pub was everything I'd thought it would be. The windows were covered with thick drapes and there was a small stage in one corner with mirrors at the back at ground level, set at an angle so's the punters could get a good look at the strippers' twats from every direction. There was a twin deck set up next to the state, with huge speakers either side. The whole place was painted black and the carpet was filthy and dotted with lumps of dried chewing gum. The lighting was dim and the place stank of stale beer, and I'd bet the glasses were dirty. All in all, a regular south-London gin palace catering to the *demi-monde* big style.

It was too early for the clientele to have roused itself; there was only one solitary drinker at the bar, and a huge barman in a black waistcoat and red bow-tie behind it, catering to his every need.

I went and ordered a bottle of Beck's and declined his offer of a glass. After a swallow, I said, 'Chris Grant?'

'In the office.' He poked his finger towards the back of the pub where I could dimly see a sign that read OFFICE, which saved me the bother of asking for further directions.

I left my beer on the sticky counter and headed for the sign, but before I could reach it a behemoth of a bloke in evening dress, with cropped hair except for one cowlick at the front, stood up from the chair he'd been sitting in, his back towards me, so I hadn't noticed his presence, and shouted, 'Oi! What's your fucking game?'

That just about done it for me. I'd been fucked around, threatened, lied to, had half a ton of scaffolding dropped on my head and shot at. Now this cunt was shouting at me, and I'd had enough.

'Do what?' I said as he came towards me, his knuckles almost dragging on the floor.

'You can't go in there, you cunt.'

'Don't call me that,' I said as mildly as possible, and put my right hand behind my back on to my gun butt.

'I'll call you what I fucking like, you cunt,' he said, and I grabbed him by the front of his greasy dinner jacket with my left hand, drew my gun with the other and stuck the pistol in his face.

'Don't disrespect me, you fucking piece of shit,' I yelled. 'Who the fuck do you think you are, you fuck?'

He looked wide-eyed at the gun as I turned him again and shoved him face forward against the bar and kicked at his feet. 'Spread 'em, you fuck,' I said. 'Wider.' I grabbed him by his cowlick and slammed his head on to the wood, and my bottle spun across the top showering foam.

The barman reached down and picked up a sawn-off Louisville Slugger from its hiding place behind the bar. I grinned, screwed the barrel of the Colt into the bouncer's ear and cocked the hammer. 'Drop it, you cunt,' I shouted at the barman, 'or I'll blow this fucker's head off and he'll die in his own shit, then I'll shoot you. You want that? Do you? I've done it before, believe me.'

He obviously did because he dropped the baseball bat on to

the floor. I leant forward and said into the bouncer's ear, 'Chris Grant. Where is he?'

'I'm right here,' said a voice from the shadows at the rear of the pub. 'You want to talk to me?'

44

Grant was exactly as Melanie had described him. Tall, dark, slimy, and I bet he was a wow with the ladies. At least ladies of a certain type.

'I assume your name's Nick Sharman,' he said, standing there all casual and elegant in fawn linen with a pink button-down shirt and a colourful tie.

'You assume right,' I replied.

'You don't listen, do you? I thought you'd been told to keep your nose out of my business. Still, now you're here you'd better come on in, and leave George in one piece, if you don't mind.'

I imagined George was the bouncer, so I let go his hair, hammered him in the kidneys with the butt of my pistol and stood back. 'Can't get the staff,' I said.

'It is a problem,' said Grant; then to his two employees, and the one customer who had watched the whole performance like it was an extension of the in-house entertainment. 'Just relax, everything's fine.' Then back to me. 'Come on through, Mr Sharman. Would you like a drink?'

'Yeah,' I said. 'Mine got spilled. I'll have another Beck's. By the neck.'

'A Beck's and a brandy, Eugene,' he said to the barman. 'The good stuff.'

'Eugene,' I echoed. 'Nice name.'

Eugene gave me a glare that said if I'd've asked for something in a glass he would've spat in it. Which was exactly why I hadn't.

Grant led the way through past the 'office' sign and I followed, still carrying the Colt, and found myself in a long corridor that sloped gently upwards towards the rear of the pub.

We went into a comfortably furnished room that was as neat and clean as the bar was grubby. Grant took a seat behind a large, empty desk with three video monitors on a shelf behind it, two showing views of the bar area, which is how come he knew I'd been outside raising a riot, and the third of what looked like the outside of the back of the pub shot from a high angle. He pointed me towards a leather swivel chair in front of the desk, exhibiting a flashy, gold Rolex on his right wrist as he did so. 'You can put that away now,' he said, indicating the gun.

'I'll just hold on to it, if you don't mind,' I replied. 'Eugene might get ugly. Or more ugly.'

'That would be difficult,' said Grant drily. 'But please yourself.'

I sat where he'd pointed, and a moment later Eugene came in with the drinks, set them on the desk and left. Grant picked up his glass and toasted me and I did the same with the beer bottle in the hand that wasn't holding the gun, letting my sleeve ride up to show him the Rolex I was wearing. He noticed.

'So what can I do for you, Mr Sharman?' he asked.

'I think you know.'

'Refresh my memory.'

'I'm looking for this woman,' I said, putting down my beer and taking Sharon's picture out of my pocket. 'Sharon Miller. I believe you're acquainted.'

He shrugged non-committally. 'Why?'

'Her husband wants her back.'

'Does he now?'

I nodded.

Grant took another sip from his glass. 'Why does he want that?'

'He's got a kid. Kid needs Mommy. That's nature.'

'He couldn't keep her before.'

'Maybe things have changed.'

'How?'

I wasn't about to tell him about the lottery win. Twelve million was rich even by this bloke's blood, so I just shrugged.

'You see,' he went on, 'Sharon has expensive tastes.'

'I've heard about her tastes,' I said. 'And how you pander to them, and how she pays you for what you supply.'

'And how would that be?'

'On her back mostly, I imagine.'

'You have a very poor opinion of me, Mr Sharman. Sharon got into certain bad habits. I was appalled. Subsequently we parted company.'

'So where is she now?' I asked.

It was his turn to shrug. 'I told you we parted company. She moved on. She went with the four winds.'

'Where?'

Another shrug. 'I don't know.'

'When?'

'Months ago. I have a fast turnover of women.'

I imagined he did.

'Tell me,' he asked after a minute's silence. 'How did you find me?'

I didn't answer and he smiled. 'Wally. I should never have trusted him.'

'I told you,' I said. 'You can't get the staff.'

He nodded in a companionable way, and it struck me that under different circumstances we could have been friends. Of a sort.

We sat there together, looking at each other and comparing Rolexes. His was newer than mine, and shinier. But I bet mine cost more. I always say you can tell the measure of a man by the Roller he wears, but then I'm a shallow bastard, everyone says so.

Eventually I said, 'You've tried to have me killed.'

'I don't think so. If I had you'd be dead by now.'

I grinned. 'Someone pushed scaffolding down on me on Sunday and someone shot at me Monday afternoon.'

'Maybe they meant to miss. A warning.'

'You'd know that better than me. I had some verbal communication about that on Monday too. But then you'd know all about that.'

'And you chose to ignore the good advice you got, by coming here and assaulting members of my staff.'

'I think your staff can take care of themselves. Besides, I don't like warnings.'

'Who does?'

'No one. But I'll tell you one thing, and you can take it any way you like, I'm going to keep on looking for Sharon, and I don't want any more warnings. Get me?'

'You talk pretty tough.'

I showed him the gun I was still holding. 'And I know how to use this.'

'But you're all on your own.'

'True. But so are you right now. No backup today.'

'But I won't always be on my own.'

'By the state of the people you use, you might as well be.'

'Despite their eccentric appearance the people I use are good at what they do.'

'I was going to ask you about that,' I said.

'What?'

'I can understand Freeze or whatever his silly nickname is. He's just your common or garden out-of-date rent-a-thug. Probably used to be a teddy boy with a flick knife outside the

Roxy. He's not the one that interests me. It's the other one. Albert. What's his story?'

'We're all out of date, Mr Sharman,' said Grant. 'Except maybe for those kids you've seen running round the pubs on your search for Sharon. Yes, my people have been watching you look. It's a small community round here. Word soon gets about. But those kids will be out of date in ten years' time too. Drinking the same drinks, listening to the same music, and some of them even with the same women. So Freeze may be a bit old-fashioned, but still effective. But as for Albert. Now he's a very different animal.'

'Animal is right,' I agreed.

'I'll tell him you said that. He'd probably like to talk to you about it.'

'Yeah,' I said. 'I've heard all about Albert. From our mutual friend Wally. When things get dull I suppose you and Eugene and George see how fast you can change his Pampers pads.'

'Things rarely get that dull round here.'

'They're going to get more exciting from now on, believe me.'

'I'll do that,' he said coolly.

'Do.' I got up and went out of the office, and through the pub where both George and Eugene gave me looks that could microwave a steak, and out of the pub and back to the car.

45

I sat behind the wheel and considered my options. It was still early and I imagined that if Grant ran the place he was in for the evening. I didn't fancy sitting in the cramped front seat of the jeep until midnight or later to wait for him, but I needed to know where he lived and if Sharon was with him. So what else could I do?

Then I had a stroke of luck. The kind of stroke of luck that private investigators who are condemned to sit alone in little cars all evening with only a packet of cigarettes, Talk Radio and an aching bladder for company pray for. For who came strolling round the corner but Grant himself, all alone. I watched as he went to the driver's side of a smart, bright red 7-Series BMW and operated the remote locking and alarm device. Now what were the chances of that happening? Especially as I was keeping an eye on a dark blue Mercedes.

Sweet, I thought as he got in and started it up, and I did the same to the jeep. Not that it was the ideal vehicle to follow another one in, being all chrome and metallic paint with its white convertible top that stood out like a whore in a nunnery.

But you gotta use what you got, as Joe Tex almost said, so I dropped in two cars behind the Beemer as it went into the one-way system at the Old Kent Road and headed north towards the Elephant, turned right under the flyover at the Bricklayer's Arms and on towards Tower Bridge.

We ended up outside a sprauncy new development of luxury apartments with a riverside view that had been converted from another old warehouse at Shad Thames. Grant locked up the BMW and went inside without looking back once. I do like a man who has complete confidence in his actions.

I stopped the jeep and sat and listened to the radio and wondered if I was wasting my time, until he came out about fifteen minutes later with a blonde on his arm, who I recognized from the photo I'd been carrying for the last few days.

It was Sharon Miller, all tarted up like a dog's dinner, but somehow, even from a distance, looking more than a little discombobulated, as if she'd been at the cooking sherry all afternoon. But I knew better.

They ignored the car and walked the short way to some poncey restaurant that a fat cunt who'd been big in the sixties and was massive now, both financially and physically, had opened south of the river where the hounds hang out, and went inside.

I gave them ten minutes to look at the menu, then quit the motor and followed. I pushed through the front door and a Sloaney girl sitting behind a desk marked RECEPTION looked at my faded jeans and battered leather and said breezily, 'Can I help you, sir?' When what she meant was: 'If you haven't got a reservation, you sad bastard, piss off. And maybe even if you have.'

I gave her a big smile that I didn't feel and said, 'I'm meeting some friends. They've already gone inside.'

'Name?'

'Grant.'

As she looked down to check her reservation list I walked straight through the double doors inside to be met by a fey-looking geezer in a Paul Smith suit and a collarless shirt done up to the neck. I hate collarless shirts. 'Sir,' he said.

'Party name of Grant,' I said. 'Over there,' and I pointed to where Chris and Sharon were seated by a window looking over towards Tower Bridge.

'That's just a table for two,' he protested.

'I'm not eating,' I said. 'I just want a word,' and I body-swerved past him ignoring his protests.

I walked up to them, nabbed an empty chair from the next table and sat down.

'Evening each,' I said. Grant looked amazed, and Sharon hardly noticed. She was chasing a black olive round her plate, and had the look of a smackhead who'd just shot up, which is what I imagined she was.

'What the hell?' said Grant, as a waiter arrived.

The waiter said to me. 'Hello. My name is Sean and I'm your waiter for this evening. The specials are—'

'Save it,' I interrupted. 'I've just lost my appetite.'

'I'm sorry,' said the waiter.

'Piss off, Sean,' I said. 'I've got business here.'

He stepped back, looking as happy as a hitchhiker in a hailstorm at being spoken to thus, and I said to Grant, 'I thought she was off with the four winds, Chris.'

'You'd better go, Sharman, or I'll get the man to call the police,' he said by way of reply.

'And explain this whacked-out bitch. Do me a favour, Chris.' The other punters were starting to take an interest in our conversation.

Then the *maître d'* arrived. 'I really must protest, gentlemen,' he said. 'Please keep your voices down.'

'Fuck off, you,' I said. 'I'm talking here.'

'I beg your pardon.'

'Don't. Just fuck off. Go into the kitchen and think about preparing an onion marmalade or whatever you serve here.'

He stepped back, looked round and beckoned, and I saw a couple more waiters, plus a couple of beefy chefs heading our way and I said, 'Come on, Sharon. Walkies.'

She looked at me as if she hadn't heard, and Grant said, 'I'm warning you.'

'Save it, pal,' I said. 'Trouble with cunts like you is that you think you're fireproof.'

I stood up and pulled Sharon with me, and she came with no resistance. I expect by then she was used to being pulled around by strange blokes. Grant made to get to his feet too so I showed him my gun and he stopped half in and half out of his seat. I tugged Sharon across the floor to the amazement of the other diners, and the staff went for me. I fired once into the ceiling, a cloud of dust spilling across the sweet trolley.

'Leave it boys,' I said. 'You ain't paid enough to die for the strawberries.' And I dragged Sharon through the doors out of the building and bundled her towards the car.

But I didn't know what the fuck I was going to do with her next.

46

Like I said, now I had her I didn't know where to take her.

I could hardly return her to her loving husband, mother and baby in their brand-new house in the state she was in. There'd be a lot of explaining to do if I did. And Grant knew where my office was, so it stood to reason he knew where I lived, so that was no good either.

There was only one place I could think of, and one pair who might take us in. The Sisters of Mercy in Notting Hill Gate.

I pushed Sharon into the passenger seat of the jeep and strapped her in tightly. She didn't say a word. And, wouldn't you know, it had started raining again. I ran round, jumped behind the wheel and took off with a screech of rubber and a fishtail from the back wheels on the wet surface, even though the car was in four-wheel drive.

When I turned over Tower Bridge, I heard the scream of a siren and a police car skidded into the road I'd just come out of. I wondered how Chris Grant was going to talk himself out of that one.

And then, on the other side of the bridge, when another cop car with its blues and twos full on dropped in behind me, I wondered how I was going to talk myself out of *this* one.

So once again I decided that discretion was the better part of valour and I slammed my foot hard down on the gas and the jeep took off.

I headed down Tower Hill into Byward Street, jumping lights as they came, faked a left turn into Eastcheap but powered down Lower Thames Street instead, under the tunnels there, along Upper Thames Street, thundered through the underpass under Blackfriars and back into the rain on the Embankment, still heading west.

I rocketed along on the far right of the road overtaking cabs and cars with my headlights on full beam and my hand hard down on the horn, much to the chagrin of every other road user going my way. The copper was still behind me and I was armed and that wouldn't look good on a charge sheet. I shot under Waterloo and Charing Cross Bridges and, without indicating, pulled on to the right side of the bollards at Northumberland Place, where the lights were against me, and went into a broadside heading for Trafalgar Square, the four-wheel drive keeping the motor on course, praying that the traffic wasn't too heavy ahead.

It was. Bollocks! With the police Rover as close to my back bumper as if it was on a tow bar I jumped more lights and headed up against the traffic again, and across the square making pedestrians puddle jump to avoid death or permanent injury.

Then it was down Pall Mall, past the soldiers on guard and up into St James's Street, across Piccadilly into Albermarle Street, where fuck me if a police van didn't join in the chase.

The three vehicles splashed through the thickening downpour into the back streets of Mayfair, round Grosvenor Square, and I for one was beginning to get sick and tired of the whole thing. Sharon, on the other hand, just sat with her eyes staring vacantly through the windscreen and didn't say a word.

As I went across Oxford Street into Duke Street and skidded into the service road at the side of Selfridges, the van driver lost control, spun out, whacked into a bollard and almost turned over. In front of us I saw a cab turning left into Baker Street. I smashed into the back of it, sending it sliding into the traffic to a cacophony of horns and a tinkle of glass on tarmac, cut across Baker Street, and against the traffic again into Portman Mews, bombed all the way to the end, turned left, the wrong way, into Portman Street and round into Oxford Street on the wrong side of the road, making cars and buses slip and slide in the wet all the way down to Marble Arch and into Bayswater road still on the right of the roundabout there.

When I dared to look in the mirror I realized that somewhere in that craziness I'd shaken off my other pursuer. Maybe I hadn't lost it after all, I thought with a grin, and wished that it was Melanie next to me and not the semi-comatose Sharon Miller.

I took the first right I could off the Baze and lost myself round Sussex Gardens until eventually I hit Westbourne Grove and knew where I was again.

I pulled up outside the warehouse, left Sharon staring into eternity and beyond and rang the bell on the front door. It was answered in a few seconds. I didn't know if it was Matty or Maddie, they sounded so alike, especially through the distortion of the entryphone speaker. 'It's Nick,' I said. 'I need some help.'

'Come on up.'

'I've got somebody with me.'

'Who?'

'The person. I was looking for. She's in a bad way. She needs help more than I do.'

'Bring her up too.'

The buzzer sounded and I opened the door then went back for Sharon. 'Come on, sweetheart,' I said and helped her unprotesting body from the car and half walked, half carried her to the lift. As it slowly ground its way up I wondered what the hell I'd got myself into this time.

Maddie and Matty were waiting when the lift arrived, both

dressed in jeans and T-shirts. 'Hello, girls,' I said when the door opened. 'Sorry about all this.'

'Is she strung out?' asked Maddie when she saw Sharon.

'On Mars,' I replied. 'Do you have a spare room?'

'At the back.'

'Is it lockable?'

A nod from Matty.

'Listen, I've got nowhere else to go. Can we stay for a few days until she straightens out?'

'Of course.'

'It won't be pleasant,' I said.

'We've seen people go cold turkey before,' said Maddie.

'And there's some nasty fuckers after us. Including Old Bill I'm afraid. And your jeep is on the PNC.'

'PNC?' said Matty.

'Police National Computer. Is the car registered to this address?'

Matty shook her head. 'It's not registered to any address, as far as I know.'

I didn't press her for more information. I knew I'd be wasting my time.

'Nobody will find you here,' said Maddie, with such confidence I believed her.

'You're marvellous,' I said.

'Come on,' said Matty, 'let's get her to bed. She'll sleep for a bit, then it'll get bad.'

But how bad I wasn't to know yet.

47

The girls took Sharon into the bedroom and put her to bed. She didn't seem to mind. She didn't seem to mind much. I figured that if I'd brought in half a dozen donkey-dicked psychopaths and set them on her, she'd just accept it. I didn't like that. It took away some of her natural dignity, and Chris Grant was the culprit.

I remembered the little boy who'd given me his Action Man. Would you want to see your mother like that?

And that led me to wonder what to do about Miller. Should I tell him now that I'd found Sharon, or should I leave it until she was more presentable?

The girls came back and Maddie said, 'She's sleeping for now. We'll make her some tea for when she wakes up. She'll be climbing the walls soon and it'll help.'

'Thanks,' I said. 'Listen. I'd better get the jeep stashed away before some keen young copper spots it. And by the way I owe you a bit for bodywork repairs.'

'Don't worry about it,' said Maddie.

'Who did this to her?' asked Matty.

'A nice man from over the river.'

'He should be shot. Why?'

'I think she earns him money.'

'Not a pleasant way to make a living.'

'It takes all sorts. How long will she sleep?' I asked.

'Till she wakes up,' said Matty, which was a big help.

'And then?' It occurred to me that in all my time on the

planet I hadn't had a lot of experience of people going cold turkey. It made me feel kind of inadequate.

'And then she'll make a lot of noise and probably mess her pants,' said Maddie. Maybe there was more of it in Notting Hill Gate. 'And then she'll want to fix up. She'll do anything for skag. She'll lie, cheat, fight. Anything. But eventually, if we keep her here, she'll be clean.'

'How long?' I asked.

'A week. Ten days. It varies.'

'How come you know so much?' I asked.

'Just lucky, I guess,' said Matty.

I went downstairs, pulled the jeep into the courtyard and locked the gates. Action Man was still sitting on the dash and I grabbed him and took him upstairs with me.

'What's that?' asked Maddie.

'Just a souvenir,' I replied. 'Is Sharon OK?'

'Only time will tell.'

So we sat down to wait.

I woke up alone in the living room with my feet up on the sofa and a blanket thrown over me, and what sounded like a banshee throwing a house-warming party down the hall.

It was Sharon. By the time I got to the bedroom Maddie and Matty were already there.

Sharon didn't look too cool. Her previous calm had gone. She was pale and sweaty, wearing a T-shirt with the duvet pulled up tight to her neck, but she was still shivering and the room smelled of faeces and disinfectant.

'She messed the bed,' said Matty.

'Who the fuck are you people?' said Sharon.

'I work for your husband,' I said. 'I'm a private detective. The girls are friends of mine. They took us in.'

'A private detective?' Sharon stared in disbelief. 'Working for my husband?'

I nodded. 'He hired me to find you.'

'Ray did? My husband? That's crap. Ray's an unemployed builder from Romford. He doesn't have a pot to piss in.'

'Things change, Sharon,' I said. 'He's got money.'

'What did he do? Win the lottery?'

She saw the look on my face.

'*No,*' she said. 'How much?'

'A lot,' I said.

'Christ.' Then something occurred to her. 'Where's Chris? Did you shoot him? I remember a gun.'

'I didn't shoot him,' I replied. 'I shot a hole in a restaurant ceiling.'

'That's right, I remember.' Suddenly her face spasmed. 'God. I feel ill. I need the toilet.'

'Come on,' said Matty. 'I'll help you.'

She assisted Sharon out of bed where she immediately doubled up in pain and let out a gasp. 'Fuck this for a game of soldiers,' she said. 'I need some gear.'

48

'Come into the kitchen,' said Matty, when they had gone. 'I'll make some more tea. It'll make her feel better if she can keep it down.'

Whilst we were waiting for the kettle to boil, Matty said, 'Have you ever thought about the human condition, Nick?'

'All the time,' I replied.

'It's sad, isn't it?'

'Sometimes.'

'Most time.'

'If you say so.'

'Just look at that poor woman out there, for an example.'

'I know,' I said. 'She's been taken for a ride, but it's not too late, is it?'

'No. As long as she wants to stay clean.'

'As far as I know she doesn't even want to *get* clean. I kidnapped her out of a restaurant. It was all I could think of doing. I don't know anything about her.'

'You know some things.'

'I know she ran out on her husband and child, went off with a scumbag with a few quid who turned her out as a whore and got her hooked on smack, not necessarily in that order. She's not exactly the Virgin Mary.'

'But her husband wants her back.'

'A fool in love.'

'Better that than not to love.'

'A romantic thought, but not to love is not to be hurt.'

'You're very cynical, Nick.'

'What I've seen of life so far has made me thus.'

She smiled. 'You know what they say about cynics, don't you?'

'What's that?'

'Bruised romantics.'

She started to make the tea as the kettle whistled.

'I know one thing about her, Nick.'

'What's that?'

'She's your responsibility now.'

'I guess so.'

'But you're not someone who takes to responsibility, are you?'

'Not in a big way.'

'I thought not. But from knowing you I imagine you've had a lot of experience with women.'

'Too much.'

'But you're alone now.'

I didn't need reminding. 'Yes,' I said.

'How many women do you think? Altogether?'

I thought about it. Jesus. Too many. Some I couldn't even give names to, and I don't just mean one-night stands, although there'd been too many of those. I mean women I had relationships with, if you could call them that. 'I don't know,' I said.

'I thought so,' she said as she poured tea into a china mug. 'Well now, although we're willing to do what we can, you've got to look after Sharon. It won't be easy. It won't be pleasant. But it's your job. You took on responsibility for her when you took her out of that restaurant. So why don't you make a start and take this tea into her. She doesn't even know who you are. Go on, Nick. Do something useful for a change.'

She handed me the cup and left me standing in the kitchen on my own. She was right, of course. It was time I did something useful. Maybe it would make up for some of my mistakes in the past. Or even the present . . . I thought about Judith up there in Scotland living with a family I'd only ever met a few times. And I thought of my first wife, now buried in a plot in north London next to her husband and child, and my second wife Dawn, dead too, with our unborn daughter in Greenwich Cemetery, and my eyes misted over. Shit, I thought. Come on, you old bruised romantic. Earn your money. And I took the cooling cup of tea and went to find Sharon.

49

She was back in bed when I walked into the room, which no longer smelt of bodily functions but rather of spring flowers out of a can. Maddie, who was sitting beside her, smiled, got up and went out without a word. Those sisters sure knew how to put someone on the spot. 'Hi,' I said to Sharon. 'My name's Nick. I think we should talk. Do you feel up to it?'

'Where am I?' she asked through teeth gritted in pain. 'Am I dreaming? I want to go home.'

'No,' I replied, and put the tea on the table next to the can of air-freshener. 'You're not going anywhere. Not right now. Just drink this. I'll make you feel better.'

'What is it?'

'A sort of herbal tea. It'll do you good.'

'Only one thing can do me good,' she replied. 'I need a hit.'

'No, Sharon,' I said. 'No more hits.'

'Who are you to tell me what I can have?'

'A concerned individual.'

'Bollocks!'

'If you say so, Sharon. But all the cursing and swearing in the world won't change what's happening.'

'And what is happening?'

'I'm going to get you sorted. Off the gear and back in the real world.'

'You can't keep me here. This is kidnapping.'

'Call the cops.'

'I would if I could get to a phone.'

'That's precisely why you won't. Get to a phone that is.'

'I could scream.'

'The walls are thick, there's no one else in the building, and the building is behind high walls. Only we would hear, and after a bit you'd get tired of hurting your throat.'

'You think you're clever, don't you?'

'No. Anything but. If I was clever I'd never have got involved in all this.'

'Where's Chris?'

I looked at my watch. I'd only been asleep for a little while although it seemed longer. 'Possibly just finishing an interesting chat with some coppers from Tower Bridge nick. I think the *maître d'* at that restaurant called nine-nine-nine.'

She changed the subject. 'Is it true about Ray?'

'What?'

'Winning the lottery.'

'Yes.'

'And you're really a private detective?'

'Yes?'

'I thought that was only on TV.'

'No.'

'And he's hired you to find me?'

'Yes,' I said again.

'Well, you've found me. I want to see him.'

'Not until you get well. There's another party involved. A three-year-old boy. I'm not having him see you in this state.'

'Liam,' she said.

This time I nodded.

'You know him.'

'We've met. He asked me to find you. Made me promise.'

'I've been bad to him.' Junkie's remorse.

'Yes, you have.'

'But I'll be better.'

'In more ways than one, Sharon. Now drink your tea.'

I picked up the cup and offered it to her but she knocked it out of my hand, sending hot liquid up the wall. I picked up the pieces and said, 'I'll get you some more, and if I have to pour it down your throat using a funnel, you'll drink it. Get me?'

'You could always try,' she said. Then her face spasmed and she broke into a sweat that I could almost smell. 'Oh God,' she wailed. 'I need the toilet again. Help me,' and once more the room filled with the stink of faeces.

50

I got her to the lavatory, which I'd already checked for sharp objects or anything else she could use as weapons, and waited outside until she came out all white-faced and shaking. 'You fucker,' she said. 'You can't do this to me.'

'Don't take bets on it, Sharon,' I replied calmly. 'You'd lose.'

She took a swing at me then, but it was pretty ineffectual and I just stepped away as she spun round and hit the wall with her back and slid down, the nightie she was now wearing rucking up, so I could see her nakedness underneath. I didn't want to look, so I averted my eyes. 'Get up,' I said. 'I'll get you back to bed.'

'I'm not moving.'

'Shit, you're not,' and I caught her arm, hauled her to her feet and pushed her into the bedroom.

'Don't you touch me, you bastard,' she wailed. 'I don't want you touching me.'

'We agree on one thing anyway,' I said, and I shoved her on to the bed and threw the duvet over her.

She lay down and looked at me with hatred in her eyes. 'I'll get you,' she hissed, 'if it's the last thing I ever do.'

'Take your best shot. But meanwhile I'm staying here and looking after you, whether you like it or not.'

And I did just that.

And it wasn't easy. I've never thought of myself as being full of the milk of human kindness and, believe me, Sharon tested my levels to the maximum. She was a mess. God knows how much gear Grant had been pumping through her system, but it was a lot. She'd been jacking it under her armpits to keep the merchandise elsewhere looking fresh. She told me that on the first day. Showed me the tracks. At least she'd used clean needles. Apparently Grant insisted on that when she'd moved from snorting and smoking the smack to shooting up.

She was pitifully proud of that. Well, she was when her moods swung in that direction. At other times she was tearfully remorseful or as vicious as a feral cat. And her nails were almost as sharp as a feral cat's claws; I was lucky to get past the first twenty-four hours without her drawing blood. It would have been just dandy if I'd had to go for an HIV test. That was what she wanted, she told me, so I tied her hands and put plasters on all her fingernails.

And let me tell you, she wasn't keen on that one little bit.

'Take them off and I'll knock you out, file your nails down to nubs and keep you tied up all the time.' I said, when I'd finished.

'Tough guy.'

'You'll find out just how tough, if you cut me,' I said.

'I'm scared stiff.'

'Sharon. You'd better learn to get along with me. You're here for the duration. That's a fact. I don't care what you do, but I'm going to see you clean or die in the attempt.'

'I hope you do die.'

'And I love you too.'

I fed her broth that she spat back in my face. I gave her ice-cream that she threw against the wall, laughing as I cleaned up the mess. I wanted to give her a good spanking after she poured Lucozade on to the bedclothes, and while I was turning the mattress and changing the linen she stood and brazenly pissed on the floor, so that I had to clean that up too.

'Right,' I said, when I'd finished. 'You make any more mess

and you'll lie in it. Shit, piss, vomit, food, I don't give a fuck. I'll tie you to the fucking mattress and force feed you, then lead you to the fucking toilet and if you make a mess there I'll hose you down with a cold shower and leave you to dry in your night clothes. You'll be cold and miserable and begging me to help and I'll laugh in your sodding face. Get me?'

She looked away and I dragged her face back by her jaw. 'Get me?' I repeated.

She spat at me again and I lost it and clouted her round the face. She spat out some bloody saliva and laughed. 'I knew you were like all the rest,' she said. 'You fucker.'

51

I felt ashamed. 'I'm sorry,' I said. 'For hitting you. I meant the rest.'

'You wanker,' she said.

'If you say so.'

'Why are you doing this?'

'I told you. I was hired to find you. I found you. I was asked to bring you back safe. I promised I would. Right now you're not safe. Not safe for anyone. Not yourself, not your family. So I'll make you safe. Simple.'

'Chris will kill you.'

'Maybe. Maybe not. A lot have tried. Some have come close, but so far no one's quite completed the deed. Sometimes I wish they had. But I have a strong survival instinct. He won't find us here, I'm sure of that.'

'Where *is* here?'

'Just a place.'

'Listen. I need to go to the toilet again.'

'You will a lot. Now, are you going to be good?'

She nodded.

'No tricks.'

'All right. No fucking tricks. Just get me there, will you?'

I helped her out of bed and along to the lavatory again. I was going to get to know that journey very well over the next few days. I stood outside until she was finished.

She was weaker when she came out, and this time accepted my offer of soup and managed half the bowl before pushing it away. She looked a real mess, her hair stringy and dull, her face covered in sweat and her skin goose-bumped and looking like a plucked chicken. Or a turkey. Hence the name: cold turkey.

'Fancy me, do you?' she asked when she saw me looking at her.

I shook my head. 'No offence,' I said.

'I bet you do,' she said, and she pushed back the duvet and pulled up her nightie to expose her blonde pubic hair. 'Natural,' she said. 'Wanna fuck? Get me some gear and you can do what you like. Anything. I'll show you a real good time.'

'I don't think so,' I said.

'Not good enough for you, is that it?' she asked. 'You sanctimonious cunt.'

Which was quite funny really, considering what she was flashing. 'Calling me names is really going to turn me on,' I remarked.

'It does some blokes.'

'Not this bloke.'

'Little Saint Nick, is it?'

I shook my head again.

'Bastard.'

52

And that's pretty much as it went for the next few days. But pretty is hardly the right word. Sharon had bad diarrhoea and vomiting, and her nose was constantly running with mucus. Her mood swings ranged from the violent to the passive. She tried to kill me one minute and get me into her bed the next. Not that she succeeded in either.

Not that I could tell exactly how many days. I didn't go out or use the phone, even to call Ray Miller. I had nothing to say to him or anyone else right then, and I didn't want anyone to speak to me. There was no TV or radio in the loft, and I didn't see any newspapers. It was as if Sharon and I were adrift in a lifeboat. And in a way I suppose we were. A lifeboat for her at least. And maybe for me, too. The girls pretty much left us alone, as Matty had said they would, floating around the place like wraiths when they were there, and vanishing for long periods of time. They left me to take responsibility for Sharon and, in a lot of ways, for myself as well. And the strange thing was Sharon never asked about them. Never once. Not who they were, or what they were or why they were there. She just seemed to accept what was going on. Strange that. But, then, so many things were strange during that period I never really thought about it.

I had other things on my mind.

At first I wasn't keen on Sharon Miller. Actively disliked her even. To me she was just a stupid, feckless, spoilt little bitch that had got herself a load of trouble and abandoned her family. She had a mug punter for a husband who'd do anything to get her back and I thought he was a fool. But by the third day of cleaning up her mess, like a mother looking after a baby, we started to forge some strange bond. Hark at me – bonding – I'd definitely assimilated too much hippie shit from Matilda and Madeleine. Next I'd be booking tickets for Glastonbury.

I didn't trust Sharon either to start with, even with locks on the door, so I moved from the couch on to a mattress on the floor at the foot of her bed. After her initial violence and sexual bravado she tried ignoring me, but without any other stimulus, and as she gradually began to get clean, slowly she started to talk. At first it was in the form of a bitter diatribe against herself, but, gradually, as her confidence and self-esteem improved, it was about anything and everything, and I started to look forward to our rambling conversations in the middle of the night, the room dimly lit by the orange glow of London that surrounded us and came in through the un-curtained windows.

The first few days I spent on an uncomfortable chair beside her, bringing her soup and tea that Maddie or Matty had made and left for me on the stove, or Coke or Lucozade, for the thirst that seemed to be a permanent part of her recovery. But soon I moved to sit next to her on her bed and held her hand. I thought I owed her that at least.

It was my fucking idea she was there.

I'd taken her from one hell hole to another.

It was my fucking hell hole, and I thought I owed her some comfort.

But in a way it was a comfort to me too.

And then one morning she started to tell me the truth about her life.

'He made me do terrible things,' she said.

At first I thought she meant Ray. 'Ray?' I asked.

'No. Chris.'

'I imagined he had,' I said.
'You don't know the half of it.'
I agreed that I didn't.
'Terrible things with terrible men. How could he do that?'
'That's how he makes his living.'
'I wasn't the only one. The only girl.'
'I never thought you were.'
'I did,' she said bitterly.
'That's how it works.'
'He was good to me at first.'
'That's how it works too.'
'We had a real laugh. But then he started me on the smack. In the end I'd do anything to get sorted. Anything. With anyone. Do you think Ray will forgive me?'
'I don't think he ever really blamed you.'
'He's a good bloke, Ray. I really pissed him about. And my mum. And Liam.' She looked over to where Action Man was sitting on the chair I'd used at first.
'He really gave you that?' she asked. I'd told her what had happened at Ray's house on the day I'd stayed over there.
'Yes,' I replied. 'And he asked you to bring me home.'
'Do you think *he*'ll forgive me?'
'There's no question.'
'And all that money. I still can't believe it.'
'It's there,' I said. 'I've seen some of the things it's bought.'
'Once that would've been very important.'
'What?'
'The things money can buy. But now I don't care.'
'Maybe that's good.'
'I think so. All I care about now is my family.'
'And that is very good.'
And soon we were talking constantly.
'How did you find me?' she asked, one long, dark, wet afternoon.

'Luck mostly. And information, of course. And being good at what I do. And I put the frighteners on one bloke.'

'Wally,' she said.

'Not one of nature's heroes.'

'I don't know why Chris kept him around. He stank.'

'And your friend Melanie pointed me in the right direction.'

'Mel.' She smiled as she said the name. 'I haven't seen Mel in ages. How is she?'

'Looking for a chum.'

'That's Melanie all right.' Sharon looked up at me from under lowered eyelids. 'I'm surprised she didn't try and rope you in. You're just her type.'

'She did. But I had other things on my mind.'

'Such as?'

'Such as looking for you. But I've still got her number.'

'You should use it.'

'I very well might.'

'She's been a good friend to me over the years.'

'She told me she warned you off Grant,' I said.

'She did. But I took no notice. Infatuated. And glad to get out of the house.'

'It was that bad?'

'No. I just couldn't stand seeing Ray lose everything. And I wasn't very good with Liam. Some women aren't good with babies. I wasn't. Now my mum . . . You've met her, haven't you?' She was having some memory problems. Nothing too serious I hoped.

'Yeah,' I said. 'She cooked us supper at the new house.'

'That's right. You said. Now *she*'s a natural. She was always great with Liam. He'd cry all day and all night and there was nothing I could do. And then she'd come in, and in a minute he was laughing. I could never work out how she did it.'

'Some people have the knack,' I said.

'I wish I had.'

And she'd go on to tell me what else Grant had put her through. It wasn't a pretty story. Humiliation. Physical and mental abuse. The withholding of her drug privileges. Pretty much par for the course in a pimp/whore relationship. I told her not to worry. It was all over.

That I'd take care of her.

That was a laugh.

But I knew she believed me, and that brought us even closer together. It was good. I felt I had some aim in life at last.

To get Sharon off the smack.

I asked her about Albert and Freeze. They scared her, and she didn't want to talk about them, so I left it.

And of course I told her about myself too. Things I'd never told anyone else in my life. Ugly things. But I knew she'd understand. Why, I didn't know. But she did.

And it was working. Every day I saw an improvement in her appearance. Gradually she got better. She stopped smoking the sixty fags a day that the girls brought home from their frequent trips out, and she stopped begging for heroin. At first, when the withdrawal pains got too bad, I allowed her a joint in the evening, but even that became a social event rather than desperation stakes, and finally we'd both end up sitting on the end of the bed sharing the spliff and looking out at the cars speeding along the Westway beside us, in the almost constant rain that seemed to beat a counterpoint to our conversations during those strange days we were together. The night-time was the best, sitting in the dark, the drug making the head and tail-lights of the vehicles blend into lines of yellow and red like a movie on time delay.

But of course it couldn't last. Nothing does.

On the twelfth or thirteenth day, she asked for her handbag.

'Why?' I asked.

'I haven't been near a mirror for ages,' she said. 'I haven't been able to pluck up the courage. I want to see what I look like.'

'You look fine,' I said.

'Go on, Nick, there's no dope hidden in the lining, and I don't have a knife or a gun. A girl needs her things.'

I got the bag, and believe me I did check just in case she'd been holding out on me, but like she'd said there was no contraband inside. 'You still don't trust me, do you?' she asked.

'Sorry,' I replied sheepishly.

She hauled out her mirror, make-up bag and hairbrush. 'Jesus,' she said. 'You could've told me I looked like a witch.'

'You don't,' I replied. 'Now a week ago . . .'

'Funny.' She messed around with her hair and put on some slap. She looked great.

'How's that?' she asked when she'd finished.

'You look terrific.'

'I feel pretty good too. When can I see Ray? And Liam? I think I'm ready now.'

'It's up to you.'

'Have you spoken to him?'

'Not since we came here.'

'Why not?'

'I had nothing to say.'

'Not about finding me?'

'Not until you were well.'

'I am well, I think.'

'Good.'

'And he'll be worrying.'

'That's nothing new, from what I can understand.'

She pondered for a moment. 'Fair enough. I asked for that.'

'Sorry. I didn't mean anything.'

'You've been kind to me, Nick. Kinder than I deserve.'

'We all deserve a little kindness.'

'Well thanks, anyway.'

'Don't mention it.'

'So are you going to? Call him I mean.'

'That's more or less up to you.'

'Then I think it's time. Tomorrow would be good.'

'OK.'

'Tell me about the new house he's bought us.'

I'd told her a dozen times already, but I told her again. It was good to see her enthusiastic about something at last. I told her where it was and what it was like, and she almost clapped her hands with delight.

'And Liam,' she asked. 'How is *he*?'

I'd told her a dozen times about him too. But once more I didn't mind repeating myself.

'Yeah,' she said, when I was finished. 'Tomorrow would be good.'

'Fine,' I said.

But it wasn't.

I moved back to the couch that night and had a desperate dream about Dawn. Not a nightmare. Just the opposite and they're the worst. She and I were sitting, talking. And she did more or less everything that had made me fall in love with her in the first place.

You know what I'm talking about. The look, the expressions, the way she ran her finger under one bra strap. The little jokes. Nothing really, but everything.

And when I woke, my face in a puddle of spit, I expected her to be there next to me in our bed in our flat. And of course she wasn't, and the pain was as harsh as the first time I felt it.

I woke up knowing she was dead.

And it hurt like hell.

And I knew something else was wrong, but I didn't know what.

But I soon found out.

53

Maddie was standing by my bed when I came to, the remains of the dream about Dawn still clunking around in my head. 'She's gone,' she said.

'Who?' I was confused and my mouth was dry. I thought she meant Dawn and I was well aware that she was gone. Forever.

'Sharon,' she said.

I blinked and shook my head to clear it. 'What?'

'Sharon's gone,' she said patiently. 'Vanished.'

'Are you sure?'

She nodded.

'When?' I said.

'In the night.'

'I didn't hear the lift.'

'She used the fire stairs.'

'Wasn't the sodding door locked?'

'She broke it.'

'Shit.' I got up from the sofa and tugged on my blue jeans. I went to the bathroom, took a piss, cleaned my teeth and tried to think. Where would she go?

When I got back I could smell coffee brewing. Maddie was sitting on my temporary bed and I guessed Matty was in the kitchen. 'What did you do with your gun?' Maddie asked.

'In the drawer in the cupboard over there.' I pointed towards the corner.

She shook her head.

'Oh fuck,' I said and grabbed the phone as Matty came in with three steaming mugs. I grabbed one and dialled Ray

Miller's mobile number from memory. He must've been asleep too and answered groggily after seven or eight rings.

'Yeah,' he said.

'Ray. It's Nick Sharman. Have you heard from Sharon?'

'Sharman! Where the hell have you been? I've been trying to get in touch with you for days.'

'Long story.'

'Have you found Sharon? That *is* what I've been paying you for, isn't it?'

'I found her.'

'When?'

'A couple of weeks ago now.'

'And you didn't let me know. I've been going half out of my mind with worry.'

I cut him off. 'She's been sick, Ray. Very sick.'

'What's wrong with her?'

'She was hooked on smack.'

'Smack. What? Heroin?'

'That's right. I've been getting her clean. That's why I didn't get in touch. I had her in a safe house'

'*Had*! What do you mean, *had*?'

'She's done a runner.'

'*What*?'

'I know, I know. But I thought she was OK here. She seemed fine. I left her alone. I shouldn't have done that.'

'Where's she gone?'

'I don't know. I hoped she was with you.'

'When did she go?'

I shrugged, although he couldn't see it, and went on, 'Dunno. Some time during the night. She might be on her way. Did she take her bag?' I asked the girls.

'What?' said Ray, confused.

'I'm talking to the people here,' I said. 'Hold on a sec.' I covered the mouthpiece of the phone. 'Did she?' I asked.

'Yes,' said Maddie. 'It's gone.' There had been fifty quid or so in her purse when I'd looked.

'How about your cars?'

'Both sets of keys are still here,' said Matty.

'She's not driving, but she's got a cab fare, Ray,' I said. 'Keep a look out for her,' and I put down the phone before the recriminations started. I didn't tell him about the gun. That scared me. That I didn't tell him. But I didn't want to make things worse. As if I could. I knew I should've told him. But we all make mistakes. I know that better than most.

'You didn't tell him about your gun,' said Maddie.

'I know,' I replied. 'I don't think she's going to shoot Ray. But Chris Grant is another matter. I think I should go see him.'

54

When I got outside it was pissing down and even though it was mid-summer it was as dark as a November morning.

I took the red jeep this time. It was all gassed up and ready to rock and roll. The blue one was still on the wanted list.

I wasn't as well prepared as the car. I was unarmed, and not even sure what was going on. What the hell was Sharon playing at? She was clean for now and seemed determined to go back to Ray and the family and be a good girl. So why the sudden disappearance?

I was soon to find out.

I drove back down the old familiar roads through the downpour to the river, then over Lambeth Bridge and turned east.

First I went to Sharon's block in Shad Thames, but there was no answer when I leant on the bell next to the card that said, S. MILLER, FLAT NINE. At least she'd made no secret of who she was.

I hung around for a bit waiting for someone to come out, getting soaking wet for my trouble. After a minute or two the security door was opened by a bloke in a mackintosh and I caught the handle as he let it swing closed. He protested, but I shrugged him off, ran up the stairs to the second floor where there was a sign that read, FLATS 9–12, and hammered on the door of number nine, but got no reply. He followed, and I said, 'Sorry, pal. Girlfriend trouble.'

'This is a private dwelling,' he said pompously, 'and unless you leave I'll be forced to call the police.' He produced a mobile phone to prove his point.

'I said I'm sorry,' I said. 'I'm going.'

'I'll see you off the premises, and make sure you don't do this sort of thing again.' I almost expected a 'my man' at the end, but at least he had the sense not to force the issue, as I might have put the telephone he was holding where the sun didn't shine. But instead I just raised my hands in surrender and walked back down the stairs and out into the street. Let him have his moment of victory, I thought. He'd be telling all his mates at the office for weeks, how he'd seen me off. Good luck to him.

I splashed back to the car and headed for Grant's pub. If she wasn't there I didn't know where she'd be.

I drove round the block and saw the Beemer that Grant had been driving the night he'd taken Sharon to the restaurant, and parked up a couple of spaces behind it. I got out and took a stroll, getting even wetter. The pub was all closed up and looked deserted, but appearances can be deceptive.

I tried the front doors but they were locked. The pub was on a corner and at the back of it, running maybe twenty yards down the side street, was a brick wall about twelve feet high topped with rusty barbed wire. Set into the wall about halfway down was a pair of double doors for delivery access. These were firmly bolted too, and also topped with wire, but they weren't as high as the wall and the wood was warped and split and stuck out far enough to give me hand- and foot-holds. I knew I was asking to get my collar felt, but, what the hell, I had to try to get inside. I waited until the street was empty and pulled myself up and over, only ripping one knee of my Levi's and the skin beneath in the attempt. I dropped down on the other side and looked round. It was the typical back of a typical old boozer. An outside Gents painted scabby green, with a single bulb behind rusty wire over its door, piles of empty bottles and casks waiting for collection, the blank back wall of the building broken only by a couple of filthy windows at second-floor height and an ancient-looking burglar alarm box just below them. There was cracked concrete sprouting with weeds at ground level, with a set of splintered cellar doors, padlocked closed, set flush into it, and the door to the back of the pub was dead in front of me.

The only thing that wasn't typical was a shiny red Jaguar XJ6 saloon with tinted windows parked nose in. Now who the fuck does that belong to? I thought.

But I wasn't going to find out standing where I was. I had to get inside. I tried the back door first. Locked tight.

Then I investigated the cellar doors. They were loose and dangerous looking to anyone wandering about after dark. I gave them a tug and could clearly see down into the darkness below through the gap between them.

I squatted down, got a firm grip on the edge of the outside door and pulled as hard as I could until I could almost hear the muscles on my back creak. Then suddenly, with a crack, one of the hasps broke, the padlock spun off, the door flew upwards nearly smashing me in the face and I ended up on my backside. I waited for the alarm to start ringing, but it remained silent, which meant that either the door wasn't connected to the system or, more likely, someone *was* inside and it was switched off.

I hung about for a moment to see if the racket I'd made brought anyone running, but the pub remained quiet, and I lowered myself down into the cellar. Luckily there was a ladder arrangement which the barrels rolled down, so it wasn't a straight drop.

The light from outside wasn't enough for me to see to the far end of the cellar, but fortunately I had my Zippo in the pocket of my jacket and I thumbed it alight. By the flickering light from the flame I made my way across the floor, avoiding the barrels and cases that were littered everywhere, and found another door at the far end. This one was unlocked and I pushed it slowly open and found myself at the bottom of a flight of wooden steps.

I climbed them slowly, trying to be as quiet as possible and pushed the door at the top open gently too.

I recognized the corridor that led to Grant's office and I crept along it, wishing that Sharon hadn't taken my gun, feeling half naked without a weapon of some kind. There was a light under the door of Grant's office and I could hear voices from inside. I put my ear against the woodwork to try and make out who was talking.

I could hear two voices. One was definitely Sharon's and the other I was sure was Grant's. They didn't sound too happy, and I thought it was time someone else got into the party.

'Here goes nothing,' I whispered to myself, and I slammed open the door, stepped inside and said, 'Mornin' all.'

55

Another mistake.

Oh shit! I thought as I looked round the office, and realized who the Jag parked out back belonged to.

Sharon and Grant were in the room OK, but they weren't alone. Sitting on the sofa that backed on to one wall, as cosy as two cockroaches on a turd, were Adult Baby Albert and Mr Freeze. Freeze was holding a Beretta nine semi, fitted with a silencer, the barrel resting across one thigh, but pointing generally in my direction. Albert was cuddling some fancy target pistol, almost certainly a .22, with an integrated noise suppressor, and the magazine in front of the trigger guard. It was all carbon fibre with a polished wooden butt, sculpted to fit his podgy hand.

Grant looked up at me without surprise. 'Perfect,' he said. 'Now the party's complete.'

'Mr Sharman,' said Albert. 'Come on in. We've been expecting you. You look like you could use a towel.' He wasn't wrong. I was soaked and my clothes were dripping on the floor. It was cold too, and I felt like a right mess. Have you ever noticed that in films when someone gets wet, in the next scene their clothes are dry and immaculate? In real life it's not like that, believe me.

I continued dripping as Albert nodded to the CCTV monitors on the shelf; the one which showed the backyard of the pub was on, the other two were blank. I'd forgotten all about them. They must've been watching me since I climbed over the gate. How many more mistakes could I afford to make?

'I'll send you a bill for the cellar doors. If you live that long,' said Grant, who produced my pistol from his jacket pocket. 'Come for this, did you?'

'I came for Sharon,' I said.

'Sharon's going nowhere.'

'What do you say to that, Sharon?' I asked her.

'I'm sorry,' she said.

'Don't be,' I said to her. Then to Grant. 'Just let her come with me and we'll forget about what happened. She's had a rough time since you last saw her. She's off the smack and just wants to go back to Ray and her boy. She wasn't thinking straight this morning.'

'She came to kill me,' said Grant. 'Can you believe that?'

'Easily.'

'Seems I'm not Mr Popular this morning.'

'Are you surprised?' I asked. 'After what you put her through.'

He smiled.

'So what happens now?' I asked.

'Now we get very rich,' said Grant.

'What?' I said.

Grant smiled a cheesy smile and I knew.

'You didn't tell him, did you?' I looked at Sharon.

But of course she had, and Grant confirmed it. 'She couldn't wait,' he gloated. 'Twelve million. What a windfall.'

'But it's not her money,' I said. 'It's Ray's. You don't think he's going to pass it on to you, do you?'

'It's not hers *yet*,' said Grant. 'But she's still his wife. If anything fatal happens to hubby, then she gets the lot.'

'Oh please, Chris,' I said disbelievingly. 'Do me a favour. It won't look at all suspicious, will it? You know. Ray finds Sharon and suddenly dies after he's just won a fortune. What with her past known associates like you three beauties here, I mean. And what about me?' Although I knew that too, and wished I'd stayed in Notting Hill.

'Come on, Nicky,' said Albert. It was Nicky now. I've never been fond of that derivative of my name. 'What do you think happens to you? And it's your own damn fault. Nobody asked you to follow her here.'

He was wrong about that. Indirectly little Liam had asked me to.

'So tell me,' I said. 'What's the plan?'

'Something like this, I think,' Albert replied, and Freeze turned his gun slightly and shot Grant through the chest, causing him to drop my gun and knocking his chair back across the carpet on its castors until it bumped gently against the far wall.

Sharon put her hands to her ears and started to scream. I didn't blame her. I felt a bit like screaming myself and I hadn't just seen an old lover shot dead in cold blood.

Albert slapped her hard round the face and she stopped screaming as if a switch had been thrown, but I could still hear the echoes of her cries bouncing round the room and, when I think about it now, I still can.

Then Freeze turned the gun on me and I saw his finger tighten on the trigger, and Albert shouted, 'Not him, you fool. We need him.'

56

But Freeze's finger kept tightening, and I could feel my sphincter tightening too in direct ratio. Then he growled, 'He's had the flowers. It's his turn now. He's got to go. He's a piss-taking nuisance and I'm tired of him.'

'Later, you bloody fool,' ordered Albert. 'I said we need him. He can get Miller for us.'

I saw the expression on Freeze's knobbly face change as he considered his partner's statement, and he loosened the pressure on the trigger and lowered the gun; I suddenly realized I hadn't been breathing and took a big gulp of air. 'Now why the hell did you kill him?' I asked, and my voice was shaky.

'Simple,' said Albert. 'This is going to be a case of "When thieves fall out".'

'What thieves?' I asked.

'You and Grant, of course,' he replied. 'We don't want little Sharon here implicated in the death of her husband. You and Grant conspired to kill him and split the cash. Then things got out of hand. You came back here and had a row and shot each other. The gun that killed Miller will be the same one that killed you, and will be found in Grant's hand.' He held up the fancy pistol he was holding. 'It'll be a shame to lose it. I've grown very fond of it. Made by Hämmerli in Switzerland. Perfect for close-in target work. But I daresay with all the money that'll soon be floating around I can afford another. Maybe two. The one that Mr Freeze is holding will be found in your hand, complete with your fingerprints. A simple shoot-out.'

'And what do you think Sharon will have to say about that?' I looked at her. She was white and shaking and just about ready to fall apart.

'Sharon will go along with what we say,' said Albert. 'She has two hostages to fortune. Her son and her saintly mother. If we two are implicated, believe me, they won't live to see another sunrise. And nor will she. Simple as that.'

'Simple as that,' I said. 'A lot of things could go wrong with that plan. Look at the state of her. How long do you think she'll be able to hold it together?'

'Long enough, when she's had a nice little hit of smack.'

'You fucker.'

'I'll ignore that jibe.'

'Ignore it or not, you'll never be able to carry it off.'

'Well, fear not, Nicky,' said Albert. 'Whatever happens, you won't be around to see it.'

A nice thought. 'And what do you mean I can get Miller?' I asked.

'Just that,' he said. 'I want you to call him.' He went to Grant's desk and picked up his mobile phone.

'I can't do that,' I said.

'I think you can,' trilled Albert. 'I really think you can. And do something about that, Freeze,' he said, gesturing in the direction of Grant's body which was still sitting in the chair, although he'd slipped down somewhat and now stared sightlessly at the ceiling. 'It bothers me. And then get the persuader from the car.'

I didn't like the sound of *that*.

Freeze handed Albert his gun, went and got Grant's chair and wheeled it out into the corridor. Then I heard him open the back door and go outside. He was back within a few minutes, rain spots on the shoulders of his jacket, carrying the largest pair of bolt cutters I'd ever seen, which he put on Grant's desk.

I was beginning to like it less and less.

'Sit down,' said Albert, pointing the gun at me. 'On the sofa.'

'What's going on?' I asked.

'We want you to phone Ray Miller, make a meet,' he explained.

I shook my head. 'No. I'm not going to get him to come out and be killed. No way.'

'Way,' said Albert. 'Sit down.'

I shook my head again, and Freeze picked me up bodily and threw me on to the sofa. Then he took his pistol back and held it next to my ear whilst Albert picked up the cutters and knelt beside me. 'What the fuck . . .' I said.

Albert leant forward and started to open the buttons on my jeans with his fat fingers. 'No,' I said and pulled back.

'I'll blow your brains out,' Freeze threatened. 'Sit still.' He put one massive hand around my neck and forced me further down on to the seat until I couldn't move. Albert finished undoing my trousers and stuck his hand into my shorts and pulled out my penis. The feel of his fingers on my private parts almost made me retch.

'What are you doing?' I said.

'You'll see,' he said, and stroked my cock which was trying to shrink to nothing. 'All this fuss about such a little thing. What do you think, Sharon?'

I wouldn't mind, but he was adding insult to injury.

'Get on with it,' Freeze hissed.

He stood back up, picked up the cutters from the desk and opened them, and I saw that the blades were stained and rusty. Christ knows what they were stained with. I didn't like to think.

Very carefully he put the cutters against my groin, catching my dick between the blades. Fucking hell, I've got to tell you my bowels nearly went again, my whole body was bathed in sweat and I was trembling, despite my best efforts not to.

'Now make the call,' whispered Albert, and I saw that his hands were shaking too. 'Or else.'

'He'd like to do it,' said Freeze. 'He's done it before.' He held out the phone.

'Why should I?' I asked. 'If you're going to kill me anyway?'

'Simple,' said Albert. 'There's more than one way to die. Quick or slow. If you make the call I promise you I'll make it as painless as possible when it happens. But if you don't, I'll cut off your prick and leave you to bleed to death. It will be both painful and prolonged. Then we'll just find another way to get Miller, and your bravery will be wasted. It's up to you.'

'You cold-blooded bastards,' I said.

'Dial.'

So I did.

Believe me, any man would.

57

Ray answered quickly. He must've been sitting on the phone. 'Sharman,' I said, and my voice almost broke as Albert nipped my skin with the sharp blades of the bolt cutters.

'Have you got her back?' he demanded.

'Yeah.'

'Where is she?'

'Not on the phone, Ray,' I said. 'Let's make a meet.'

'Where? When?' His eagerness was almost pathetic. Especially considering what the Rover Boys had in store for him.

I wanted to scream for him to run. Get lost. Anything. But I also wanted to keep my wedding tackle in one piece, and I knew that if I *did* warn Ray by word or deed, I'd be bobbitted in the most unpleasant way. I didn't underestimate Albert's propensity for cruelty for a second. And as long as I was in one piece and not bleeding all over the floor there was still a chance I could retrieve something from the mess I'd found myself in. No. Put myself in.

'There's a pub in Waterloo, on the Cut,' I said. 'The Blue Posts. Nearly opposite the Old Vic. Know it?'

'I'll find it.'

'Meet me there at twelve.'

'Will you have Sharon with you?' he asked.

'Just meet me, Ray. I'll explain everything.'

'Is she all right?'

'Twelve o'clock,' I interrupted and killed the mobile. Then

I looked at Albert. 'You are a stone-cold bastard, do you know that?'

Albert pulled the cutters away from my groin and said, 'Do yourself up, love, you're getting me all excited.'

I didn't have to be told twice, but believe me, right then and there I made myself a promise: if I had to die in the process, I was going to get even with that fat fool and his ugly mate.

'We've got a couple of hours to kill,' said Freeze, not even noticing the irony of the statement. 'I think I'll watch a little TV. There's good stuff on at this time.'

'Do what you bloody well like,' Albert snapped. 'I'm going to get a drink.'

'What about the staff?' I asked. 'Won't they be here in a minute? And the customers?'

'The pub's closed until further notice,' said Albert. 'Refurbishments. I'll take care of that.'

'It'll look funny,' said Freeze as he fiddled with the real TV next to the monitors and found the programme he was looking for.

'Nearly as funny as Fat Boy here in that little girl's dress and a nappy,' I said.

'Say what?' said Albert, turning round.

'Don't be coy,' I said. 'There's nothing to be ashamed of – getting in touch with your feminine side. I tried it myself once, but I tore my tights.'

'Freeze,' said Albert.

Freeze reached over and gave me a careless clout round the head with one of his great big hands. 'Shut up,' he said. 'Talk when you're spoken to.'

So after Albert went out to the bar, Sharon, Freeze and I sat and watched Richard and Judy for an hour or so until it was time to go.

Before we left the pub, Freeze trussed Sharon's hands and

feet up with gaffer tape that was used to fasten down the wires from the PA system in the bar. He gagged her with the same stuff and my last view of her was her blue eyes looking at me beseechingly. Freeze pulled a tight pair of black leather gloves over his hands, and he and Albert took me, the bolt cutters and the mobile phone out to the Jag. Freeze shoved me into the back and cuffed my wrists to the ring bolt that was welded to a brace under the back seat. They were obviously prepared for this sort of situation.

'Sit there and shut up,' he said as Albert waddled over and opened the double doors leading to the street, and closed them again after Freeze had backed the car out.

58

Their nasty little plan went like clockwork. Ray Miller was waiting in the pub like we'd arranged. I knew he would be. He couldn't wait for any news I had of Sharon. I spotted his motor parked outside on a meter. It was pouring with rain by then. Pissing down. Albert made me use the mobile he had with him to call him out into the street. He didn't need much convincing. Truth to tell I didn't need much convincing to sell him out either. One mention of the bolt cutters in relation to my private parts did it, although I'm ashamed to this day that I was such a coward.

Albert and Freeze had been singing along to the radio on the journey to Waterloo like a pair of kids on an outing. Oldies but goodies on Capital Gold. The Tremeloes, Vince Hill, Stevie Wonder. You name it, I had to put up with it. And neither of them would've passed the audition.

Ray Miller walked out of the pub like a man going to his own wedding rather than his own funeral. I could hardly bear to watch as Freeze sent the car rocketing across the road and Albert dropped the window and popped three bullets from his silenced pistol into Ray's chest, which knocked him to the ground, sending up splashes of water from the puddles he'd been standing in. I twisted round painfully in my seat and watched out of the back window at his still form receding into the distance as Freeze sped away and round the first corner he came to.

Shit! After everything I'd been through to try and reconcile Ray and little Liam with Sharon, it was all for nothing. Just a bloodstain or three on a cold, wet pavement in the fag end of south London, which would be washed away by the rain before a few hours had passed.

I tried to justify myself to the two killers in the front seats as we sped back to Albany Road but it didn't work.

Not for me and not for them.

I would've shed a tear for Ray on the journey, but none came. My eyes were as dry as Mr Freeze and Adult Baby Albert's hearts were cold.

59

All the way to the pub Albert and Freeze were laughing and joking in the front. At least Albert was. Freeze was a bit slow on the uptake, and didn't get a lot of the punch lines. It was still raining. Harder than ever if anything. Freeze got out of the motor, opened the doors at the side of the boozer and then drove the car in, getting a good soaking as he closed them behind us. 'What now, Albert?' he asked, when we were parked and the engine was switched off.

'Now we go and tell the richest woman in south London that she's come into her fortune,' replied the fat man.

'You're never going to get away with this,' I said.

'On the contrary, Nicky,' said Albert. 'She still has the remains of her family to protect. I think she'll go along with whatever we say to save them.'

'She dumped her family once before, don't forget.'

'And bitterly regretted it. She's a mother after all. And mothers, whatever their faults, will ultimately protect their children. Especially when their lives are on the line.'

From the way Sharon had talked when she'd been in Notting Hill I knew he was right.

'What about him?' asked Freeze, giving me a dirty look.

'Leave him here for now. He's safe. We'll deal with him later.'

They got out of the car and ran through the rain to the back door of the pub, leaving me to ruminate on my fate. It didn't look good.

The rain beat an insistent tattoo on the bodywork of the

Jag, and without the air-conditioning the inside of the windows soon misted up and reduced my world to a few square feet of leather upholstered luxury, which I imagined would be the last thing I saw before they killed me and got on with their lives. I sat there, feeling sorry for myself, until the driver's door opened. From my cramped position at the back I didn't even bother to look round. 'Just get it over with,' I said. 'And make it quick.'

'Make what quick?' said a familiar woman's voice and I almost broke my neck looking round.

It was Maddie.

'What the fuck . . .' I said.

'Nice welcome,' she said, climbing into the driver's seat and pulling the door to behind her. She was soaking wet with her hair plastered to her head.

'How did you get here?' I asked.

'We came looking. We found the jeep parked round the corner, saw you come in here with those two nasty guys you told us about. We waited, then came over the wall.'

'Where's Matty?'

'Hiding over there.' She gestured through the windscreen.

'Good. They've got a camera somewhere. CCTV.'

'I understand the concept,' she said. 'What have they done to you?'

'Nothing much so far. Just got me trussed up like a chicken dinner and threatened to cut off my manhood. But they've just killed Sharon's husband, and they've got her prisoner inside. They're trying out some scam to get the lottery winnings.'

'Oh, Nick, I'm sorry. You were quite fond of him weren't you?'

'I've known worse blokes. But we've got no time for that now. Those two will be coming to finish me off soon.'

She reached over and felt the handcuffs. 'How are we going to get out of this?' she said.

'On the floor under the front seat,' I said. 'There's a big pair of bolt cutters. That's what they threatened to use on my dick. Get 'em.' She fumbled around and came up with them. 'Slice the cuffs off,' I said.

It took her all her strength, but the blades were strong and the handles were long enough to give her leverage. After a bit of a tussle I was left with just a set of matching bracelets as souvenirs. 'Come on, let's go,' I said, and we left the car and ran over to where Matty was waiting behind a pile of beer crates.

60

We crouched down together as the rain tumbled from the sky, soaking us to the skin. 'Thanks for coming,' I said to Matty. 'I owe you one. Another one,' I added.

'Didn't you know we would?' She was smiling.

I shook my head.

'You don't know who we are, do you, Nick?' she said. A question she'd asked before, but I still didn't have the faintest idea what she meant by it, so like before I ignored it. This was certainly no time for guessing games. Instead I said, 'Sharon's inside with fatso and his mate. They've killed Grant and they just shot Ray Miller down in the street.'

'We should call the police,' said Maddie.

'No,' I said. 'It was my fault Ray was murdered. I set him up. And I owe him too. I'm going to get Sharon myself. You can do what you like.'

'You haven't got a weapon,' said Maddie. 'And they're armed.'

'I know they're armed. I'll take my chances. Anyway I've got these.' I held up the bolt cutters that I'd brought from the car. And then something struck me as I looked at the crates of bottles all around us. 'And that's not all,' I said. 'Wait here.'

I jumped up, ran for the car and tried the boot. It was locked, so I inserted the blades of the cutters into the gap between the lid and the bodywork and twisted them hard. The boot popped. Inside was the spare wheel and as I'd hoped a plastic can. I picked it up and shook it and heard liquid slop inside. I slammed the boot shut, praying that the boys inside weren't watching the TV monitors, and ran back to the girls.

I unscrewed the top of the can and crossed my fingers it wasn't water for the radiator, but I smelt petrol fumes and grinned through the rain running down my face. 'Delicious,' I said. 'Grab a couple of bottles. And be quick in case those bastards spotted us.'

They did as they were told and I filled four bottles to their necks. 'Either of you girls got any tampons on you?' I asked when they were full.

'This is hardly the time to worry about our menstrual cycles,' said Maddie.

'I'm not worried about the time of the month,' I said. 'Have you?'

'I've got some panty pads, I think,' said Matty, and opened the shoulder bag she had slung round her neck and rummaged around in it. 'Here.'

She gave me a packet with half a dozen pads inside and I ripped off the plastic backing from four of them and folded the pads themselves and forced one into each of the four bottles filled with petrol. 'More absorbent, see,' I said as I splashed petrol on to the cotton, trying not to get any on my hands or clothes.

'You coming with me or not?' I asked when the Molotov cocktails were ready.

'Course we are,' replied Maddie.

'Cop for these then,' I said to the girls, who took two each. I picked up the bolt cutter, and thus armed I tried the back door of the pub. It was open this time, Albert and Freeze not having bothered to re-lock it when they went inside.

Careless boys, I thought and we went inside too.

61

We crept down the corridor towards Grant's office, past his body which still sat in his office chair staring at the ceiling. I saw both Maddie and Matty wrinkle their noses in disgust. I was in the lead and I stopped for long enough to close his eyes. He deserved that respect at least, whatever he'd done. I pressed myself flat against the wall when we came close to the office door. It was shut. I touched my finger to my lips and beckoned for them to follow me, past the door and on into the bar, hoping no one had switched on the interior cameras.

I pulled them both close into a huddle and whispered, 'We've got to try and separate them. I need to get one of them in here and get his weapon.' I looked round, then at the front door that was hidden by thick curtains. I walked over to it and pulled the curtains back. As I remembered from that morning, when I'd tried to get in, there was a bell push outside. I ran my hand up and found where the wires came through the jamb, ran up the frame and away to the bell somewhere inside the building.

I beckoned the girls over and explained my plan. 'I'm going to make this bell ring,' I said. 'Hopefully they'll think it's a customer or member of staff or a delivery or something. The pub should've been open hours ago, but obviously it's not. If the bell keeps ringing, with a bit of luck one of them will come and tell whoever it is to get lost. You two get down behind the furniture. I'll hide behind the bar and sort whichever one it is when he comes out. Don't show yourselves unless you have to. You've got your lighters?'

They nodded in tandem and showed me their twin Zippos.

'OK,' I said. 'Use the bombs if you need to and only if you need to. But for Christ's sake be careful. They might both come out together, and they've got guns and they're stone killers. I don't want to lose you girls.'

'You won't,' said Maddie, and they ducked down behind a pair of banquette benches, one each side of the door, whilst I got to work.

I pulled the bell wire away from the clips that held it against the wood and split the strands, then stripped an inch or so from each with my thumbnails and touched the wires together. There was a tiny spark and I heard the bell go at the back of the boozer. Bingo! I looped the wires together, getting a small shock for my troubles as the wires connected, left them, grabbed the cutters and ran and ducked down behind the bar.

The bell ran naggingly for a minute, then two. Come on, come on, I thought. I heard a door open down the corridor, then slam, and muffled footsteps on the carpet and Freeze's unmistakable voice shouting some obscenity. From my position behind the jump I saw his trousered legs pass the gap in the bar heading towards the door. He was alone and I breathed again. I popped my head up as he dragged the door curtain back and shouted, 'What's all the bleedin' racket?' He worked the bolts on the door, tugged it open and stuck his head out into the rain ready to berate the caller further.

But of course there was no one there, and I saw him look up and down the street and then at the bell push outside as I silently came out from my hiding place and crept across the floor towards him. He let the door slam shut and pulled the curtain away. Then he saw the wires loosely tied together and stiffened.

By then I was about two yards from his back. 'Knock, knock,' I whispered, and as he spun round I raised the bolt cutters above my head, one handle in each fist, and like some kind of matador from hell going for the kill I smashed the blades down into his chest. They penetrated with a crunch and he staggered back ripping the handles from my grasp.

He stood perfectly still for a moment, the cutters protruding from his body, and then with a roar he grabbed the handles himself, pulled them out of his chest cavity with an obscene plop followed by a spurt of blood and tossed them into the corner where they hit the wall and bounced across the stage. He looked at me with an eye-popping stare, reached down and pulled the silenced Beretta from inside the waistband of his trousers and brought it up to bear on me. Shit! I thought and started back-pedalling fast, when Maddie and Matty got into the act.

As Freeze pulled the trigger and a round whizzed past my ears, they popped up from their hiding places, a Molotov in one hand and a Zippo in the other, lit the fuses and threw the bottles. Maddie's smashed against the wood of the door jamb sending a spray of molten petrol over Freeze, and Matty's smashed into his head, broke, and covered him in fire.

He dropped the pistol he was holding and screamed as he began to dance around the bar showering liquid flames with every step. He found the curtains over the door and dragged them down in an attempt to dampen the fire, but only succeeded in setting them alight.

I bent down and grabbed the gun. It was an awful sight seeing him crashing round the bar in agony, and I fired twice into the fire to try and finish it. But the bullets only seemed to make him crazier, and he threw himself across the floor leaving flaming footsteps on the carpet as he went, until eventually he crashed against the bar itself, tripped and fell to the ground, where after a final convulsion he lay still.

62

By then the fires Freeze had started while he was stumbling about were beginning to claim the bar. It was an old pub. Ancient really. One of those from Victorian times that hadn't been demolished by bombs during World War Two – or the town planners who had made more of a mess of London during the fifties, sixties and seventies than any thousand Nazi pilots could in their wildest dreams. It was frightening how fast the flames were spreading as they devoured the material that lined the interior of the building.

There was no hope for Freeze as he lay where he'd fallen, his clothes welded to his skin that was black as coal, where it was visible, and stank of cooked meat, enough to make me want to spew. 'We've got to get Sharon,' I yelled at the girls. 'Get out,' and the bottles behind the bar began to pop and their alcoholic contents made the fire rage even harder.

We ran out of the bar into the comparative coolness of the corridor, but I knew that wasn't going to last. The whole building was going to burn to the ground, and all inside with it, unless we got out quickly. I shoved the girls down towards the back. 'Outside,' I said. 'And get clear.'

The door to the office was still shut and I hammered on it with the silenced end of Freeze's pistol. 'Albert,' I screamed, standing to the side, out of the line of fire. 'It's Sharman. The place is burning down.'

It was just as well I had stepped back for all I got for my troubles was two bullets through the wood and a face full of splinters.

'Come on, man,' I yelled again as the smoke began to drift round my legs and I could feel the temperature rising. 'I'm not kidding.'

One more round came through and I knelt and tried the door knob. It was locked and the smoke caught in my throat and I coughed harshly and felt my eyes fill with tears. I checked the clip in Freeze's gun. With the bullet in the chamber I had ten rounds left, and I shot shit out of the lock then kicked the door open, still keeping as far out of the line of fire as possible.

The smoke drifted into the room. 'Albert,' I yelled. 'If you don't get out now you'll burn to death.'

'And Sharon with me,' he yelled back. 'What have you done with Freeze?'

'He's dead,' I said.

A hail of bullets slammed into the wall opposite and the sound of the fire was getting louder behind me. The smoke was billowing so hard I could barely breathe.

'Give it up, Albert,' I spluttered.

'Fuck you.'

'You'll fry.'

'Like hell I will. I'm coming out and I've got your girlfriend with me. Throw down your gun or she gets it.'

'I don't think so.'

'Do it, Sharman,' and Albert appeared at the door using Sharon as a shield, although she only covered the centre of his bulk. She still had her hands tied and the gag in her mouth, but he had cut the tape on her ankles. The revolver that she'd taken from me was in Albert's right hand against the side of her head, the hammer cocked and his finger hard on the trigger. 'Don't think about it,' he warned me. 'You try a shot and I blow her head off. Now, throw down your gun.' I couldn't risk it. Even if I managed to put one into the flesh that Sharon didn't cover, he could blow her head off and get a shot at me too, so I dropped Freeze's pistol at my feet.

'Kick it away,' he said, and I concurred.

He came all the way out in to the corridor. I moved away and could feel the hair crisping on the back of my neck from the heat of the fire, and steam was rising from my wet clothes, fogging my vision.

'It's been nice knowing you,' he said and he moved the barrel of the revolver away from Sharon's head and aimed it at me. 'Sucker.'

Then from behind him I heard a voice call his name and I could've sworn it was Grant's. Albert stopped in his tracks as the voice called his name again, this time from closer, and he turned, and past him, through the smoke, I saw Grant, still in his chair, rolling down the slight slope in the floor from the back of the pub. In each hand he had a beer bottle full of petrol with the wick made from a sanitary towel burning merrily, and I swear for the split second I saw him, his eyes were wide open and there was a smile on his face.

Albert screamed at the sight, let go of Sharon and fired repeatedly at Grant until the bottles exploded and the chair ran on into Albert's great bulk streaming flames behind it. Just then the force of the fire from behind me blew the wall next to where I was standing on top of me. And I remember thinking what a waste all the efforts to get Sharon back alive had been, and that was all I do remember.

63

I woke up to the clatter of dishes and registered an institutional green ceiling and white walls. My throat felt like it was coated with carpet tile. I blinked and looked round. I was in bed in a hospital room. There was a TV mounted on the wall. It was on, showing an afternoon soap with the sound turned down low. Next to the bed was a locker with a vase of flowers and a bowl of fruit on top. Someone was sitting by my bed in an armchair. I blinked again, not believing my eyes. 'Judith,' I croaked.

She looked up from the magazine she was reading. 'Dad,' she said, dropping the paper to the floor and jumping to her feet. 'You're back.' And she really sounded pleased.

'What happened?' I said. 'I thought I was dead.'

'No. No. Of course you're not. Don't be silly.' She went to the door.

'*Nurse*,' she shouted.

'Gimme water, please,' I begged.

She came back and poured liquid from a plastic jug into a plastic glass and held it to my lips. I drank greedily, then pushed it away. 'What the hell's going on?' I said.

A young nurse came into the room. 'Welcome back, Mr Sharman,' she said. 'How are you feeling?'

'OK,' I said. 'Hungry. Thirsty.'

'That's good.' She took my temperature, pulled a 'not bad' face and said, 'I'll get the doctor to look in in a minute. You seem fine.' And she left.

'Judith,' I said when she was gone. 'What happened?'

'You got some minor burns and a bump on the head. At that pub, remember?'

'Sort of.'

'You were lucky. Someone called the fire brigade. They found you and a woman. Sharon Miller. You were looking for her. Do you remember that?'

'Course I do.'

'They got you out,' Judith went on. 'Seems you saved her life.'

'Did I?'

'Sure. You're a hero. You rescued her from those murderers.'

'Blimey. Did I?'

'Course you did.'

'How long have I been here then?'

'A week.'

'Bloody hell.'

'And there's someone else here to see you.'

'Who?'

'Hold on, I'll get him. He's been here every day. He's just getting a drink.' She ran out of the room and left me alone.

Within two minutes she was back with a companion. I blinked again. It was Ray Miller. 'It can't be,' I said. 'You're dead.'

'Not quite, Nick.'

'I don't believe this. I'm getting all confused.'

'Don't be. It's quite simple.'

'So what happened to you?' I asked. 'The last time I saw you you'd just taken three bullets in the chest outside that pub in Waterloo in the pissing rain. It *was* you, wasn't it?'

He grinned and nodded. 'After what you told me about those two killers, and when you sounded so strange on the phone, I dug this out,' he said, then leant down and brought up a large plastic Selfridges' bag from under my bed, put his hand in it and pulled out what at first looked like a khaki waistcoat. 'I kept this from the Falklands,' he explained. 'My old flak jacket. It saved my life there and saved my life here. Look.' He held it up like a clothes salesman and I saw that it was torn in several places. Old tears by the looks of them. And there were three new holes, clustered close together where his heart would be. 'He was a good shot,' he said. 'Nice pattern. Knocked me down and I got some bruising, but nothing serious. Twenty-two calibre, a piece of piss.'

'Just as well he didn't go for a head shot.'

'You're not wrong.'

I had to laugh. 'I don't believe it,' I said. 'That's outrageous. Ray, I'm so glad. You don't know what they did to me to make me call you that day.'

He looked serious all of a sudden. 'Yes I do,' he said. 'Sharon told me. I don't blame you. I'd've done the same.'

'I don't know about that. You're a war hero, remember?'

'Not when my nuts are in a vice,' he said, then reddened and looked at Judith.

'Sorry, love.'

'I do know what you mean,' she said.

'How is Sharon?' I asked.

'She's getting better. Like I said, she made a full statement to the police. Told them how you got her away from Grant, cleaned her up, and then rescued her again when he re-captured her.'

'He didn't,' I said. 'She went back to kill him.'

He looked at Judith again. 'Do you want me to go?' she asked.

Then he looked at me. 'No,' I said. 'She stays. Anything we've got to say she can hear.'

'Fair enough,' said Ray Miller. 'I know what she was going to do. She told me. But we don't have to tell the cops the whole truth, do we? Not after what Grant put her through. If

I'd've known I would've tried to kill him myself. The cops want to see you too. If your stories back each other's up, who's to know any different? Anyway, I've instructed my solicitor to be present. He's very good. And very expensive. I've got his card here.' He handed me an oblong of pasteboard printed in gold. 'He expects you to have some memory problems after that knock you took,' Ray went on. 'Know what I mean?' And he winked. 'He'll take care of everything and send me the bill. And talking of bills . . .' He took an envelope from his inside jacket pocket. 'There's a cheque in here for ten grand. That's the least I owe you. And I've instructed him to pay for this room here for as long as you need it. And any consultancy fees or anything else that might come up.'

'That's very generous. But you already paid me out front to find Sharon.'

'Forget it. Call it a retainer. This settles the account.'

'And what about Albert?' I said. 'The last thing I remember is him hiding behind Sharon and getting ready to shoot me.'

'Sounds like what I've heard about him. Dead, I'm afraid. No, I'm glad. He perished in the fire along with his two mates. An accident. That's what Sharon said.'

'But the other two had bullets in them.'

'Grant was murdered by Freeze, then you killed him in self defence. Then Albert shot at Grant's dead body. And all this was happening while the building you were in was burning in an unfortunate fire.'

'Sounds a bit far-fetched to me.'

'But it's the truth, isn't it? That's what Sharon told me.'

I had to agree. It was more or less.

He placed the envelope on the bedside table. 'Take this,' he said. 'You deserve it. Take your daughter on holiday. She's been worried.'

I looked at Judith and she smiled and I could see the love

in her eyes and I knew everything was going to be all right again, even though it had taken a bump on the head and a week in hospital for me to make it so. Suddenly I remembered. Maybe I *was* having trouble with my memory. 'What about the girls?' I said to Miller.

'What girls?'

'Matty and Maddie. Twins. They helped get Sharon through cold turkey and turned up at the pub. They got me out of the car. Without them I'd be dead. And God knows what would've happened to Sharon.'

'Sharon didn't say anything about any girls.' He looked genuinely puzzled. 'Just you and her.'

'Where is she? Can I talk to her?'

He shook his head. 'No, Nick. I don't think that's a very good idea. She's still a bit uncertain. Anyway, you can't. She's gone.'

'Gone? Where?'

'New Zealand. Her and her mum and little Liam. They flew out a week ago. I only stayed till you came round properly. I wanted to make sure your stories matched. Now you're awake I can join them.'

'*New Zealand*.'

'It makes sense, Nick. All we have here is bad memories. New Zealand's like England. Same sort of climate. And it's as far away as you can go before you start coming back. We've got the money. Plenty. And we need some time together to get over all that's happened. We're going to buy a farm. A big one. Raise horses maybe. I've always fancied that. Maybe you can come and visit sometime. But not for a while, eh, Nick. Listen, I've got to go. I'll send you my new address. We'll talk.'

'No, Ray. I need to know some things—'

But just then the doctor came in and Ray left. I never saw him again, and he never did send his address.

The doc gave me the once-over and seemed as pleased as doctors ever are. Then he left Judith and me alone.

'You had another visitor,' she said as she pulled her chair up close and sat holding my hand.

'Who?'

She smiled. 'Her name's Melanie.'

I'd forgotten all about Melanie.

'She's a bit young for you, isn't she, Dad?'

'Don't you approve?'

'Course I do. She was nice. She left you a present.' She opened the drawer in the locker and took out a small parcel. 'Want me to open it?' she asked.

I nodded.

She peeled off the paper and, looking puzzled, handed me a silver referee's whistle on a leather thong. 'She said you'd know what it was for.' I laughed, though it hurt a bit, and said, 'I know what it's for.' That Melanie. What a joker.

'And what's all this about things to wear round your neck?' said Judith.

'What?'

She reached back into the drawer and brought out the crystal on its chain.

'You were wearing this when they brought you in. It's not like you, Dad. Are you turning into a geriatric hippie?'

She handed me the pendant and I felt a tiny shock as I touched the jewel.

'No,' I said. 'It was given to me for luck. And it looks like it worked too.'

64

Ray Miller was as good as his word about his solicitor. The police interviewed me a couple of days later. Right there in the hospital room with me sitting up in bed looking a little dazed and dribbling orange juice down my jim-jams the whole time. Ray's solicitor, a wide boy from Lincoln's Inn named James Walpole, had briefed me on that. He wanted me to appear a little out of it. Which wasn't difficult, as I was. He also told me to check with him before answering any questions. One shake of the head and I was just to say 'No comment'. I'd seen the papers by then and Judith had been right about me being a hero too. For the first time in my life.

There were two Old Bill. A DS Ryker and a DCI Barrett with two 't's'. He made a point of mentioning that. They brought in chairs and Walpole hitched up the legs of his immaculate pin-striped strides to save the crease and perched on the edge of my bed.

I had my orange juice ready in a plastic beaker, and Barrett said, 'Well, Mr Sharman. We're sorry to bother you here in hospital, but there are one or two things we need to clear up.'

Sorry, I thought. That's a new one. Normally the police are only too happy to see me banged up with something seriously amiss with my health. 'Whatever I can do,' I said. 'But I'm afraid . . .' I touched my temple, pulled a pained face and slopped some liquid on to my chest. '. . . My memory isn't what it should be.'

Walpole narrowed his eyes as much as to tell me to lay off the histrionics, but I was enjoying myself too much.

'On the day of the nineteenth,' said Ryker, 'you went to the Druid's Rest public house for what reason?'

'What happened on the nineteenth?' I mumbled and Walpole coughed.

'That was the day of the fire at the pub. The day Raymond Miller was shot at three times and the day that Albert Courtney, Jack Neal and Christopher Grant were killed,' Ryker said through gritted teeth.

'Chris Grant I remember,' I said. 'But the other two . . .'

Ryker gave me a dirty look. 'Courtney and Neal were better known as Adult Baby Albert and Mr Freeze respectively.'

'Of course,' I replied.

'Well,' said Ryker.

'Well what?' I asked, slopping more juice.

'Why did you go there?' said Ryker.

'I thought Sharon Miller was in danger.'

'You'd spent some time with her previously,' said Barrett.

'That's right. When I met her she was addicted to heroin. I helped her kick the habit.'

'Where did you meet her?' asked Ryker.

Here we go, I thought. Someone's put two and two together about the incident in the restaurant on Shad Thames. 'You must know Ray Miller hired me to find her,' I said.

Barrett nodded.

'I made certain enquiries and diligently followed them up and that led me to her apartment by the river. I waited for her to come out, introduced myself and she entrusted herself to my care.'

'As simple as that,' said Ryker sardonically.

'Just about,' I said. 'I told her I was working as an agent for her husband and she seemed to accept it.'

'There were no guns involved at this time?' said Barrett.

'No,' I said innocently.

'Only we had a report of an incident at a restaurant in Shad

Thames involving a young woman, a man who gave his name as Christopher Grant and another man. Armed. Who answers to your description and possibly was later involved in a car chase across London. You don't own a Suzuki Vitara convertible, registration number R143MMS, by any chance?'

'Perish the thought,' I said.

'Or know anyone who does?'

'No,' I said. 'Who's it registered to?'

'That's the problem. No one.'

'Bit naughty that.'

Walpole nudged me.

'Now Mrs Miller has made a statement to the effect that Grant kidnapped her, took her to his pub and told her that he intended to kill her husband and blackmail her into handing over most or all of the winnings he had won on the lottery. Twelve million quid or thereabouts.'

'That's about the size of it.'

'Then Neal shot Grant and you later managed to kill Neal using his own gun. How did that happen?' asked Barrett.

Tricky subject. 'I don't remember,' I said.

I saw Walpole nod and I knew I'd given the correct answer.

'Mrs Grant says he was trying to kill you.'

I shrugged. 'I believe what she says. She struck me as a truthful sort of woman.'

'Even though she's a whore and a junkie,' said Ryker.

'Sergeant,' said Walpole, 'I object most strongly to you referring to my client in such terms. And she is my client, as you know. Has been since the nineteenth of last month. Now Mr Sharman is just trying to help. You see he is still under medical care. He was struck on the head. I have a slew of eminent medical practitioners who will tell you he may suffer short- or even long-term loss of memory about events on that unfortunate day.'

'I'm sure you have,' said Ryker.

'I certainly have and will if necessary.'

'You and Miller's twelve million.'

'John. Leave it,' said Barrett.

'And Courtney shot Grant after he was dead,' said Ryker. 'Now why would he do that?'

I shrugged again. 'I don't know,' I said. 'But the place was on fire. That I do remember. Maybe he thought Grant was after him.'

'When he was already dead?' said Ryker sarcastically.

'"There are more things in heaven and earth, Horatio, than are dreamt of in your philosophy,"' I said. 'Maybe he went crazy. Maybe he always was. He liked to dress up as a baby, remember. You can't tell me that's normal.'

'Who's Horatio?' said Ryker.

Barrett sighed, and I knew I was home free. But he had to make one last try.

'And you have no knowledge of where all these guns that were on the premises came from?' Ryker asked. 'You must know that possession of a handgun is a very serious crime these days.'

'I do,' I said. 'And I don't. Know where the guns came from, that is. I don't have any truck with them these days.'

Barrett shook his head sorrowfully. 'Mr Sharman. From what we know of you, the idea of you without a pistol is like Troilus without Cressida, Rosencrantz without Guildenstern.'

Very Shakespearean, I thought. He obviously knew who Horatio was. Ryker of course looked even more confused.

'OK, Mr Sharman,' Barrett went on. 'That's all for now. You've come out of this very well. Mrs Miller has made a statement to the effect that you acted in self-defence throughout. Ray Miller held a press conference that has you as a knight in shining armour. Me, I'm not so sure, but there's nothing I can prove. So we'll leave it at that for the moment. We know where you are. There may be charges brought at a later date, but frankly I doubt it.'

The coppers were all right, as it goes. The solicitor hardly had to raise any objections about their questions. Mind you, the three that had died at the Druid's Rest were hardly model citizens and wouldn't be missed. Not by Old Bill at least.

When they'd gone I asked Walpole where the Miller family were staying, but all he would tell me was that they weren't settled yet. And afterwards, whenever I rang the number on the card Ray had given me, he was always in a meeting with a client and never returned my calls until in the end I stopped bothering.

But I had the flak jacket for a memento, and the cheque for ten grand was good, otherwise I'd believe I'd never met Ray Miller or Sharon or Angela or little Liam.

Or Melanie Wiltse, who became a regular visitor once I'd come back to the land of the living, and would continue to be one for quite a while after that.

And as for Maddie and Matty. Well . . .

EPILOGUE

I never saw the twins again. Sometimes, now, I still wonder if I ever did, or if they were just an elaborate dream or hallucination. But at night, when they haunt my sleep, I know.

When I finally got out of hospital, before I took Ray Miller's advice and went for a long holiday in the West Indies with Judith, I drove down to Notting Hill Gate to look for them. It was a filthy day, with black clouds hanging low over west London, and occasional bursts of squally rain that almost defeated the windscreen wipers on my car.

The warehouse where they'd had their loft apartment was different than I remembered. Deserted. Abandoned.

The front gates were locked and the entryphone was missing, so I simply climbed over them. The lift door was pulled down tight and fastened with a chain and padlock, and looked as if it hadn't been opened for years. Above the cover a faded FOR SALE sign was nailed.

I went round the back of the building and behind a half-full skip that stank of piss I found a door. I forced it open and climbed endless flights of concrete steps to the top.

The space where they'd lived and where I'd stayed with them was just that. A massive, filthy, empty space with broken windows, that only wild birds made their home.

No one had ever lived there. At least not for a long time. And even though I should've been surprised, I'd more or less expected it.

But there was one weird thing. One in particular amongst many weird things that had happened that summer.

In the middle of the loft space, on top of an upturned tea-chest, was a vase that contained two fresh red roses.

As I walked across the dusty floor that held no footprints except those I left behind, I saw that the flowers were moist and new and their perfume overcame the rank air.

As I reached the chest, the sun suddenly broke through the thick black clouds above London and filled the loft with a warmth and glow that reminded me of my first night there, and I smiled. They'd been real all right, but where they were now I'd never know.

I reached up and removed the chain from round my neck and touched the crystal that hung from it and draped it over the flowers.

Then, without looking back, I left the warehouse and drove home and opened a fresh bottle of brandy and drank it until finally I could sleep.